ROME TREE

A Funny Thing Happened on the Way to a Horse Race

O n the run for daring to criticize the medical profession, the Delphic Oracle and her crew stumble across Zeus on the way to a Horse Race. As if the ensuing mayhem of Werewolves being evicted from Hades, the hordes of heaven descending to kill them, and really bad-tempered Unicorns competing in a rigged race were not enough, the Trumpetus Orange with Lord Rupus Murdochious decide they too need a piece of the action.

And let's not mention the Catholics who want to burn down New Rome! Fast paced farce at its best.

Ecallaw Leachim

WARNING

THIS IS A TRUE MOCKUMENTARY

Being the unabridged story of what would have happened if Caesar had discovered the bicycle, Rome had never fallen, and we had ventured out onto a completely different time line.

We are in a world where Rome never fell.

Caesar discovered the bicycle, thus was able to get away from his assassins, and went on to thoroughly reorganize the entire world, and bring it under Roman control. Roman stayed as the ruling power right up to the present day.

In Book One, the Delphic Oracle created a new sensation, which required a lack of killing things when you wanted to see what the Gods were thinking. It changed everything! The use of rubber chickens instead of real ones created a bull run on the rubber market, and an entire new economy emerged.

However, the Oracle was not content with this, and started saying that ALL bloodletting was unnecessary, including the preposterous notion that LEECHES were not a medical essential. This made her hugely unpopular with the good Doctors, who harassed both she and her troupe of Un-Funny Comedians out of Canada.

And then, on the way to a horse race at Woodstockium, which was really at Bethel, madness descends.

Other Books by this author:

Psychic Nazi Hunter - Biography of Alan Wood-Thomas

Eat Your Fill / Eat Your Religion / Eat Your God Trilogy

The Book of Number Trilogy

Jermimiah Versus the Grabblesnatch

The Divinity Dice Series

Ratology: Way of the Un-Dammed

Ratology II: Who Gives a Rats?

Water: More Precious than Gold

The Borringbar War

Fragments of the Mirror

Hello Planet Earth

The Dream Electric

Rome Too / Rome Tree

Old Harry Jenkins

Psychic Nazi Hunter (Amazing Biography)

Ladder to the Moon Publications

Available on Amazon or at
www.laddertothemoon.com.au

4

Index:　　　　　Page:

Introduction — 9
Escape to New Rome — 12
The New Deal — 17
Mexico — 19
By Zeus ! — 22
Flavius Corpus — 25
Of Horses and Men — 28
New Rome Bound — 30
Olympus — 35

Part Two — 39
Werewolves — 40
The Party — 44
The Day of the Race — 47
The Godly Chariot — 48
The Day of the Hunt — 52
Time — 56
He Haw, He Hamed, He Honkered — 60
A Meeting of Old Friends — 62
Wolf Plans — 65
The Dock of New Rome — 67
Hot Tip — 69

Sling Shot to Bethel — 73
Performance Jitters — 75
Stock it to Me — 78
A Curious Revelation — 82
The Performance — 84
Utter Confusion — 87
Race Riot — 90
Aftermath — 96

Part Three — 98
The Flaming Sky — 99
The Green Door — 102
New Rome Times — 107
The Pit — 109
The Orange Principle — 113
News Wars — 116
Persnickety Perfection — 120
The Orange Revolution — 122
The Mad Parade of Bacchus — 126
New Rome Burns — 127
After the Fire — 129

ROME TOO

What if Rome Never Fell?

Ecallaw Leachim

WARNING: Parody and Madness Ahead

Don't forget to catch up with the FIRST Book in the Rome series: Rome Too. Available on Kindle and an Amazon.

ROME TREE

A Funny Thing Happened on the Way to a Horse race
Copyright M Wallace 2019

"Are you talking to yourself"

"It is the only time I get a reasonable conversation"

"It is a sign of madness"

"Majority-Minority Rule: Those in the Majority maketh the rules. But if the majority are stark raving bonkers, then the opinion of any one of them is the notion of a lunatic, and the society they inhabit is equally looney tunes. The fact that I talk to myself in an insane world only proves I am saner than the rest."

"So you are saying it's a minor problem?"

"No, I am saying I am a minority without a problem!"

"Why are we having this conversation?"

"Who said I was talking to you? I was perfectly happy talking to myself."

"Well, majority-minority rule back at you. if you are insulated from society, you are a minority, therefore your opinion doesn't count."

"So, do you think it is a problem talking to yourself, then?"

"Only when other people butt into the conversation."

"Who is to say I am not you, and that WE are talking to ourselves?"

"Hmmmm, good point. But I can see you are wearing a hat! Nice hat."

"What? The Fox Hat?"

"The hat? It's the thing you have on your head."

ROME TREE

A Funny Thing Happened on the Way to a Horse Race

COPYRIGHT 2020 Ecallaw Leachim
This book is published under the Berne Convention. All
copyright protected to the author. No prior use
without permission except for excerpts for review or
educational purposes. All enquiries via Email to:
   info.numberharmonics@gmail.com
   Published by Ladder to the Moon Publications.
   ISBN: 978-0-6484277-5-9

INTRODUCTION

ZEUS   PEGASUS

I
t is the New Age of Rome. Sacrifice has been abandoned in favor of ritual sacrifice and, as a result, a whole new way of thinking has come about. People now believe that anyone can read signs and omens and a whole lot of new tools to assist this new attitude have come about.

Bone throwing kits (using rubber bones) along with rubber chickens with fake entrails and tarot cards were now appearing in every household. Further, the number of ghost sighting went through the roof, though authorities rushed to explain these were mostly swamp gas.

Polite society requires a majority/minority rule to function. As a result, now that the majority believed in ancestral spirits, it was considered *de rigueur* to nod knowingly while some woman explained that the spirit leaning on the vegetable rack was, in fact, her beloved great grandmother that she never met. In return, when she visited your place, she would also nod knowingly while you explained about the spirit of some distant relative advising you that you had to kill your visitor.

Poltergeists were having a field day. It was the only explanation for all the money and valuables that went missing. People responded quickly to this threat by hiring experts to assess the threat of poltergiestability in their houses. The rational explanation of spirits needing things on the other side could not be argued with, yet some were suspicious it was simply, ordinary theft at work.

Yes, even when the professional poltergeist research teams were caught with said poltergiested materials, it was explained that the spirits had simply asked the investigating party to carry said items for a bit, as the spirits were tired of poltergiesting. In other words, a perfectly reasonable explanation, and it was now time to drown would-be witches to see if they floated.

Yet, while inspecting houses for valuables that spirits took made a lucrative profit, poltergiesting was as nothing when compared to Newly Minted Catholics. All the various Christian Sects had banded together, declaring that the Delphic Oracle herself had approved of Jesus, and formed a 'one religion' to go with their rather ridiculous 'one God'. You may laugh at this absurdity, but their "Pay to go to Heaven" routine worked a treat. When added with confession for your sins giving you absolution, well, the people really went for it.

This was a license for debauchery like no other. You could do whatever you wanted, confess your crimes and you get forgiven - then if you just paid a little money, you were GUARANTEED admittance to a good afterlife. No more Styx, no more paying Charan his outrageous tax but the REAL bonus - No putting up with the pessimism of Hades.

No sensible Roman could resist such a great offer. Trumpetus Orange helped the Christians in developing a better and more marketable brand. This was the one thing he knew, how to extract money from Romans. As a group, the Christians had rightfully expected to cash in on the fake ritual business, because, in their mind, they got their first. And now, thanks to the Trumpetus, they DID. They were even re-branded to become ROMAN Catholics! Brilliant move! Their obvious patriotism is what moved them out of the lions' mouths and into Trumpetus' hungry maw.

Needless to say, the new Catholics got nothing from the proceeds, as they had to pay enormous sums to Trumpetus for the franchise he sold them - of their own religion. When some Bishop asked about this, he explained "You see, before ME, you were all being hunted and fed to lions, now you are not. This is because I re-badged, re-packaged and re-labelled you." He explained, while pointing out the contracts they signed had effectively made them all his slaves. Ergo: If they wanted to argue he had the legal right to beat them.

But there were a few that DID argue and, despite being beaten, they said it was very, very unfair. Trumpetus just said, "Give unto Caesar that which is Caesar's - but he's dead, so you give it to me, OK?" It was only with such a perfectly scriptural explanation like this that everything finally settled down and it got back to business as usual.

A new contract was signed that made everyone happy. It ran as follows: *"You, the ROMAN Catholics save the Souls while I, the Trumpetus Orange, save the cash."*

However, the notion of eating a dead person, despite it being so fashionably fake, just never caught on. They got members, they got bribes to go to heaven, but the churches themselves were empty. This was very disappointing to certain members of the teaching, so, as a protest, some of these newly minted Catholics developed a nasty habit of burning things down, to encourage people to run from the fires of hell and into their various places of worship.

The greatest shift after this was political, with Lord Rufus deciding to support Trumpetus Orange, the Trumpinius Rex (The King Trumpeter - though some said he was the Kinky Trumpeter) in a bid to control the political life of New Rome. Running on the bill as co-consuls they were currently looking certain to be voted in, which was another way of saying they had bought enough votes.

Neither came from a Patrician family, so the whole city and all of the New Americas was up in arms about this change to the *Mos Maiorum* (The traditional ways). The pair had paraded on a ticket called "The New Deal" saying they would improve the lot of the needy, give money to the poor, and create new housing for those who were on the rocks. A reporter asked who exactly these needy might be, but most simply presumed that it was the Consuls, as they always needed money more than most.

However, this is but a sidebar to the real story. Poor Eruptus Non Funnius had gotten themselves into hot water yet again.

When we last left off, Rufus, Ofal, and Meridius had settled up in Canada and were doing rather well - But then the Oracle started kicking on about leeches. Common sense, you might think, but it caused a huge kerfuffle with the medical profession

Escape to New Rome

Meridius remained the Oracle, despite her absence from Delphi. She liked the New World of America and decided to stay there for a bit. Her compatriots, the Un-Funny Comedians and now famous Rufus Maximus and Ofal Biggins, were keeping her company as they escaped the ravaging mob that was after them.

"Meridius, stop looking at the moon, we have to catch a donkey!" Rufus shouted, grabbing her bag and throwing it onto the cart then running back, picking her up, and doing the same with her. Ofal was already in the driving seat with an excitable donkey who, though normally very slow, decided that living was better than dying, and got off at a cracking pace.

In past times, this had been a fairly normal event. As members of the trio, Eruptus Non-Funnius, they were often to be found (or preferably not found, as the case may be) escaping from the jeering and booing crowd that hated their performance. But of late it had been quite the opposite. Everywhere they went they had been celebrated as the architects of the New Age of Rome. People were in the streets cheering them on, all because they had invented the ritual, ritual sacrifice! This was the new invention where no animal was actually butchered in order to obtain a pronouncement regarding any or all omens from the Gods.

However, today was not one of the cheering days and more of a "we want to kill you" episode that they were erstwhile so used to. _How easily people forget all that you do for them_, Rufus was thinking to himself as rattled down the cobblestones escaping the angry mob.

The Rubber Chicken, the Rubber Sheep, the Rubber Goat, these were the new hot items that were leaving the backs of carts at an extraordinary rate. The augury business took a dive, but as the old ways adjusted, the soothsayers figured they could work with fake animals if that is what the public wanted. Which is another way of saying they junked all their principles because they wanted to eat.

To their vast surprise, the oracular pronouncements based on fake animals seemed to work out just as well, and it saved an enormous amount of cleaning up afterward. In truth, the people were entirely over all that blood being spilled on every occasion. And let's face it, birthdays, Bar Mitzvahs and burials are not really events where you want to have chicken entrails spread all over the place to tell you if it was a good or bad occasion. You could reasonably expect the signs for a birthday to be good and, conversely, those for a burial to be bad. And as far as Jewish festivities go, everyone knows there were no open Bars at their Mitzvahs, so who cared what the omens said?

It was somewhat of a social revolution, especially given that for over two thousand years the old ways had held sway. Some old folk predicted doom and damnation for all, shouting "The chickens will come home to roost!" Strangely enough, this proved to be accurate - though some would say this was because they were not scared of getting butchered by some half-baked priest anymore.

But not all was rosy. As is the way with most revolutions, there are quite a few unaccounted for deaths. People got quite excited over the whole matter and, in the early stages of this new paradigm, there were some fairly serious arguments between the old ways and the new.

Protesters would be railing against some ritual where a sheep was to be sacrificed, holding up their rubber substitute, shouting that rubber works best. Naturally, the local priest then decided that perhaps a few of the protestors would make a better offering to the Gods and did a substitution of his own. It was extremely awkward at funerals of the dearly departed where the same priest had to read an Augury.

There were also other unexplained and mysterious disappearances. The first was the presumed death of the Jupiter Optimax, who was heard screaming how much he hated the Gods and in particular the Delphic Oracle shortly after he pronounced the official ending of State required sacrifices. The Gods must have struck him down.

The second vanishing was less mysterious: Baraka Alashad disappeared soon after his extensive purchases of land in New Rome were queried and just before the subsequent bankruptcy proceedings started.

The third was Focus Maximus, which was a puzzle because no one was hunting him. But his hovel was empty without so much as a goodbye note.

Of course, there was also the chief priest of Delphi, who many believed probably killed himself, but no one knows because there was no note, only a screaming sound when he heard that the Oracle had cashed in her holdings at the Delphi Bank. It was later found a large amount of gold had disappeared with him and it was generally agreed that he had not 'technically' stolen it, but had gone to Mount Olympus to try and buy a God-hood.

Which brings us to the fifth soon-to-be-missing group of people, Eruptus Non-Funnius. Poor Rufus was SO upset - it had all been rosy, peaches and cream - But now it was back to business as usual, escaping the angry mob.

Ofal sighed. "You told her, Rufus, you told her to leave leeches well enough alone. But no, ending animal sacrifice wasn't enough. Now our nice little gig that made us pots of money is over, and it is back to scratching a living in the wilderness." Ofal was a little depressed, not because of the mob, or the leeches, but because he had found himself a very nice harem who he now couldn't see for fear of being torn to pieces.

"No point saying anything, Ofal, she is off again in the moon worlds. There is nothing for it but to hightail it out of Canadia and lie low back in New Rome for a bit. With luck, her new anti-leech movement won't have reached there and we can camp out at the House of Claudius."

"Bit pretentious, isn't it? House of Claudius, like he is some sort of Lord." sniffed Ofal.

"Well, he IS landed gentry now, which makes him a sort of Lord, you know ... But regardless, Patricians like him like to emphasis the difference between themselves and the ordinary jocks like you and me. Plus, honestly, Claudius's House sounds weird, don't you think? Like a snake got loose with too many "S's" or something." Rufus looked back at their Oracle, daydreaming away in the cart, oblivious to the danger they had just escaped. He sighed to himself, she was both their greatest fortune and greatest curse.

She is the one who elevated them to celebrity, bringing with it the money that fame adores. However, she was also the one who started predicting the end of Leeches in modern medicine. Maybe if she had offered some sort of replacement, like they did with the rubber chicken in place of the real chicken? But no, she just went on the record (in a trance of course) saying that leeches were done. THEN she went on to further announce that ALL bloodletting was done, and further, that the whole "bloody" business had been entirely pointless.

It was a slap in the face of authority. Declaring them wrong, stating that the Gods didn't care, and generally acting as if you knew better was a red flag to the punctilious bull. They started charging at the little troupe like they were enemies of the State. Which, in Canadia, meant most people would look at you with a very doubting sort of look.

The entire medical community of Canadia, for instance, started saying terrible things about them in the press. A suggestion 'was' made by one sensible reporter that they test the oracle's prediction - and that they could do this by having two patients. The good doctor would leech one, but not the other. Then you wait - Watch for a bit and see how it worked out. This was, of course, laughed at as an absurd notion. Leeches were a constant in the doctors battle against disease and had been good for two thousand years. What's more, the medical ones cost a fortune and were a significant asset in every good surgeon's practice. The Oracle was damaging the doctors hip pockets with her insults, not just their reputations.

That was when the lawsuits started and, as the lawyers turned up the heat, their bank accounts got frozen. Somewhat inconvenient when you had to pay costs and buy things like food. Yes, they still had the country houses, but you can't eat land, so as a consequence they had to get out and do performances. This was a mistake because the good doctors had decided that "Do no harm" had an exclusion clause - specifically regarding people who said bad things about leeches. They roused the mob to attack them, wanting to do away with the Oracle's anti-leech prediction for good.

"On the positive, we are out of the house and back on the road," said Ofal musing. But only for a moment, as a great lump of a creature suddenly leaped in front of their Donkey, scaring it to a standstill.

"I hear you are in need of protection!" roared the familiar and thoroughly unwelcome voice of Brutus Maximus.

"Are we?" asked Rufus who had less of a look of surprise than a glower of deep resignation.

"Indeed, the mob is out and about and are baying for blood!" roared back Brutus, oblivious to any possibility that he may be unwelcome.

"What brings you hereabouts?" asked Rufus, trying to work out how they were going to get rid of him. "I thought your Uncle sent you up to the deep North to hunt for Elk or something like that."

"Ho ho ho! Yes, a good bit of subterfuge that. No, it was the hidden mountain of GOLD I was sent to find, the El Dorado! That is why I have spent this past few years out in the middle of the frozen tundra, fighting with bears and eating raw reindeer."

"Ah, El Dorado is in SOUTH America, isn't it?" Rufus noted.

"May as well be," retorted Brutus. "No Gold Mountains anywhere up here!"

Focus Maximus probably just invented the notion to get rid of him, thought Rufus. Wisely, this is not what he said. "Your uncle vanished, didn't he?"

"Did he? That would explain the lack of letters then." Brutus' eyebrows knitted in what appeared to be a passing thought. A rare occurrence, to be sure, but it passed fairly quickly. "That would mean going to see him would be more difficult, wouldn't it?"

"Ah, yes, I would imagine so," responded Rufus.

"But this ALSO means his hovel will be vacant, won't it?" Brutus seemed quite proud he had figured out a cunning plan.

"You want to move into your Uncles hovel while he is classed as missing?"

"Only to protect his property. You never know with vandals and all that," replied Brutus, very pleased his plan was approved. "How long will it take us to get there?"

Rufus realized that a very good argument would be needed to keep Brutus from their donkey cart. "Ah, the servants there may object. And possibly his wife might as well. You may not be welcome."

"Scufflebucks and nonsense, he has no servants, no wife, and it's a hovel." Brutus was happily climbing on board as he said so. "And anyway, when does a wife or a slave have priority over the rights of a blood relative?"

"Well, in the case of a wife, always," suggested Rufus. But he was rebuffed with a scoffing wave of the hand as Brutus settled in for the long cart ride down to New Rome.

"Did you know I once rode an elephant?" he said, and without waiting for a reply, "Not a circus one either, but a proper war elephant. He was a biggun ... "

"Pardon?" asked Ofal, whose last name was Biggins. "Are you saying my relatives are elephants?"

"Glad you mentioned relatives. Have you not considered, dear Rufus, that we may be related?" Brutus queried.

"Well, no, but I do have certain nightmares..."

"You see, we BOTH have the surname of Maximus, which I didn't realize until I was told about all the kerfuffle with the assassins trying to kill my uncle and all. I never realized you were Rufus MAXIMUS, you see, and with my Uncle being Focus Maximus and myself being Brutus Maximus, well, you can easily see the connection."

Rufus now had the distinct impression that he had found a new and very unwanted relative. "Ah, it is a very common last name, you know."

"Yes, but we HAVE to be related because we DO have the same last name," Brutus explained.

"Have you considered that we might have been adopted?" Rufus tried to escape the unyielding claws of a Brutus who had decided he was your cousin. To no avail, the fellow just laughed his large and hearty laugh and camped there beside Meridius as if this was his new home.

"I love meeting relatives, you know!" he roared.

And so the adventure begins ...

The New Deal

Trumpetus Orange stood there, waving and smiling to the jeering crowd. By his side, Lord Rupus Murdochius appeared to be somewhat more aware of the extremely hostile nature of the mob in front of them, but Trumpetus kept right on waving and acknowledging them, as if they were throwing palms at their feet. "They love me, you know," he said as a matter of fact to his compatriot.

He caught the cabbage being tossed in his direction and called out, "Thank you for your contributions to the poor. But please give them to someone who actually cares." This got the crowd laughing. Rupus just looked on in amazement, the guy did this all the time. He just didn't seem to notice that everyone hated him and yet, at the end of it, they loved him.

"We all know things are not what they used to be. I look around, and I see poverty. I don't like poverty. You don't like to see poverty, because it making a mess of your nice clean streets. We want to get rid of it! (loud cheers) Poverty means fewer people buy the crap I sell. Poverty sucks! (The crowd cheers even more) Now we need to fix this and I have a great plan. I say we need to start selling the poor into slavery, which will have a two-fold benefit. First, it increases revenue to the State and, second, it gives these poor, who are usually homeless people, a place to live. Do I hear you people? Do I HEAR YOU?"

The crowd roars, though Lord Rupus is not sure that they realize what they are cheering for. The singular fact HE sees is that ALL of them would be classed as being poor, thus about to be sold into slavery. But all the roar and noise of their own roar and noise spurs them on and they cheer even more. "You see," Trumpetus says to Lord Rupus, "You just give the people something that sounds good and they buy it."

"You aren't actually planning on selling all the poor into slavery, are you?" Lord Rupus asks.

"Of course I am. All part of making New Rome great again."

"I was never certain it was all that great to begin with." Lord Rupus noted. He genuinely didn't like his running mate, but the pairing of his media control and Trumpetus's cash meant they were certain to get in - particularly as their only opposition had a few discussions with an assassins from the roadside tavern. The prospect of your imminent death does tend to put lesser souls to flight.

"This New Age craze is going big. We should cash in on it, but we need a better hook. Anything in the news?" Trumpetus has a faraway look, clearly dreaming of great things to come.

"The Oracle has made a new prediction, but this one is really crazy."

"Even better, I mean the last one about the end of Rome was not really precise, but it got a lot of press. The end of Rome, as we know it, that would have been better, but what's the new angle?"

"She is predicting that Leeches and bloodletting are done. The medical establishment hates her, and she has been chased out of Canadia." Lord Rupus was never a fan of leeches himself, but everyone knew they were part of the essential medical equipment for every doctor. They are a fixed truth, an impregnable rock upon which the medical profession stands. *No leeches?* You may as well say colds and flues weren't caused by malevolent spirits! Just so ridiculous.

Apparently, Trumpetus saw things differently. "Fantastic! This is perfect. We can go on about how the medical establishment has been leeching off the sick and helpless, sucking the lifeblood out of them, and the Delphic Oracle supports us! Beautiful, that is the next speech! And while I am at it, what we really need is a better wall around New Rome. New gates, higher wall, more guards. That is sure to get votes."

"Who the hell is going to pay for all this?" Rupus wanted to know because it sure as Hades wasn't going to be him.

"The Gauls can pay for it."

"We are nowhere near Gaul and we already have a mountain range and a sea between us and them." Rupus insisted.

"Details details. When will you learn? People don't care about the details. What they want is the big picture. What we are getting them is a NEW DEAL. Things will be different when we get in, nothing will be the same, and I love the idea of socking it to the medicos. Let's make sure we nail them and their leeches to a cross!"

The crowd was still roaring as the pair made their way from the Agora in their election chariot. "Oh, and I had a great idea, Trumpetus Tarot Cards! It is another way to cash in on the New Age thing." With this, the orange-haired creature hands a deck of cards to Lord Rupus, who opens them to find a very unique set of cards. Every one of them had a painting of Trumpetus Orange depicted on it.

"Ah, this deck of Tarot Cards only has one picture: You. It is the same on every single card, every one of them is a painting of you though with a slightly different expression!" Lord Rufus points out.

"Exactly, I am the future and this proves it! When they do readings with MY cards, all they ever see in their future is ME. I just love it!"

Looking back, this really should have been a large red flag to Lord Rupus as to just what Trumpetus intended. But at that point he was busy thinking about how expensive a crossroads assassin might be.

Mexico

Baraka Alashad and Chincino were happily ensconced at the resort strip in Cancun, Mexico. The heat from the bankers was starting to cool, which was good, but sadly so were their funds, which was not. The combination of these two factors meant a possible return was being planned. "I mostly have it worked out, but there are a few small hiccups to get past," assured Chincino to his boss. "The house is gone, the slaves have been sold off, despite the fact I traded them all into a secondary company before it all went tits up, but the good news - if you could call it that - is that Garam bought the lot. He is living in a house beside the stock market, you know, at the wall?"

"Those damn patricians have everything in their name!" cried Baraka, not really caring where Garam Marsala lived, only that he still lived, and lived in a house that HE bought. It was such a perfect plan, consign a couple of Patricians to be bonded slaves, then use their good Roman names to buy up real estate in New Rome as the prices tumbled. With everyone panicking about the end of everything, it worked brilliantly, and Baraka had snapped up hundreds of bargains.

However, once his clever plan worked, Garam and Claudius, the Patricians in questions, traded out of their Slave Status with good old fashioned bribery. With all the real estate in their name, and all the debt in his, then suddenly losing his legal claim over the real estate, he had no comeback. "I put all that damn real estate into THEIR names, but as slaves, all their chattels still belonged to me. How did they get the registrar to remove them from the Slave Lists? I mean, we know HOW, but WHO did they bribe, and how can we get to them?"

"The problem is that you are not a Roman Citizen, dearest Baraka. There is no legal response you can make to the bribe for two reasons. One, as a non-Roman you are not allowed to sue a Roman in the courts. Two, as a registered debtor, if you step into Rome, it is off to the Tarquin you go. All you can do is get them assassinated, but that doesn't get your money back." Chincino knew he was walking over glass with this subject, but it had to be done. Of course, he had a plan, he just had to survive it.

"However, there IS a way around it. You can release ME from servitude, then transfer your slave contracts with Claudius and Garum to myself. As a Greek who became a Roman citizen, I can then take the conniving patricians to court and it will then be easy for me to prove how they hoodwinked you. Once we restore them as slaves, their property is forfeit, so we get it all back."

"We?" said Baraka gloomily. "You mean that 'you' get everything."

"This is true, however, can you think of a better plan? And this way, at least one of us gets rich. But the fact is, I like you Baraka, and I will do you a deal, let's go halves." Chincino calmly made his suggestion, fully expecting some sort of murderous outburst from the African prince.

The sun, the sea, the relaxing atmosphere and the friendliness of the Mexicans had a tonic effect on the African tribal chief. He really didn't feel like killing anyone today, or tomorrow. He rather liked it here. Yes, they had to do something and killing the two patricians was his preferred option, but then he reasoned they only did what any true Roman would do: to seize any opportunity to get rich. Despite the fact he had this very day been advised that his credit at the Bank of Delphi had run out and despite the fact he wanted to murder them, he felt a grudging respect.

He knew they were greedy little pigs when he picked them up, and while he had offered the pair a house each when it all settled, why go for one house when you can get a hundred of them? "I bought them one hundred houses EACH!" he said. "TWO HUNDRED houses and I went into hock up to my eyeball to do it. They hold the titles and get the rent, while I am stuck with the bill. Even if we go halves, I am still bankrupt."

Chincino saw the opportunity. "Well how about this for a suggestion: Let's say we go halves of the net profit after the dust settles. Keep in mind, I can't do this without you, you can't do this without me. "

Baraka just looked at his slave for a bit. In truth, this was pretty much the only way forward. "So you are suggesting a full 50/50 partnership, with my debts paid off as a priority, after which I, or we, can buy and trade real estate in New Rome because of your citizenship, while I remain your official partner. It is not so bad, but this agreement is only legally binding if signed in Delphi, so we have to get someone with full authority to register our arrangement. The only person with that sort of authority in the Americas is the Delphic Oracle."

"Precisely, and as you helped her out so much, I am sure she would be happy to oblige." This was starting to look pretty good, thought Chincino.

"What is this nonsense about her wanting to ban Leeches?" He asked.

"Well, interesting stuff. Her talk about this has opened new and different opportunities. In point of fact, there is a remarkable new invention I found down here at the local witch doctors house, a thing that could make us BOTH a lot of money. It is called aspirin!"

"Aspirin?"

"Yes, a white powder that takes the place of Leeches. It thins the blood, like leeches do, and it cures headaches, just as leeches are prescribed for. Aspirin also eases aches and pains, another thing that covers what was once Leech territory. In fact, it is a wonder drug that does EVERYTHING a leech will do, minus the loss of blood. We will make an absolute killing by trading it onto the New Rome stock market." Chincino produced a small satchel that had a white power in it.

"This is Aspirin?"

"No, this is Cocaine, which even better than Aspirin. This is the SECOND product we put into the market, which will triple the profits from Aspirin."

Baraka was starting to see that a partnership might not be such a bad idea. "So how do we get back into New Rome without me getting arrested and thrown into a debtors cave at the Tarquin?"

"You are happy with a partnership deal, then?" Chincino checked before proceeding.

"Not at all, but fifty percent of something is better the one hundred percent of nothing. It's a deal Chincino, you are freed as a slave and are now my business partner. We just have to find the Oracle to register the agreement." Baraka felt a weight off his shoulders. Some part of him believed in his former slave and trusted him. "I am trusting you with my life, Chincino."

Which was a very clear way of explaining to Chincino that he was dead if that trust were ever broken. Baraka was a warlord first, a businessman second. War had just become unprofitable with the world being mostly conquered, which was why the fellow was in the Americas in the first place. There was a greater opportunity for profit there.

"Well, first things first. As chance would have it, I bumped into an old friend, the Lead Augury of Rome when I was in the markets yesterday. Talking to Focus Maximus, he happened to mention that he had foreseen the Oracle was on her way into New Rome from Canadia as we speak. If we take a ferry we will be there in a few days. But there is a small detail that complicates things: Getting you into New Rome without being arrested means I will have to pass you off as my slave ..." He waited. But nothing - No explosion of temper? This was not right, Baraka was never one to be accepting of his fate.

The huge black man continued to gaze out to the ocean. What a strange turn-around of events. From one of the richest men in New Rome to hiding under the coattails of a former slave. He sighed whilst his new partner organized a few things for the trip.

Chincino was also considering the changing tides of fortune, from a wealthy solicitor caught out in a bad deal on Wall Street, to selling himself into slavery to cover debt, to finding the Oracle, to becoming a partner to one of the (erstwhile) richest men in the new world.

If it were not for his natural pessimism, things were moving along well.

By ZEUS !

B rutus Maximus had fallen soundly asleep with the regular wobble from the donkey cart, yet even so, between snores, he continued talking about his far-off adventures in distant lands. It did not appear to bother Meridius, despite the fact he was slumped over beside her while babbling on.

"Are you back yet?" Rufus asked her. He was entirely used to her emotional and mental disappearing acts now, all of which was apparently part and parcel of the whole Oracle thing. She seemed to be coming back to them. He sighed, she was both his greatest curse and greatest blessing all rolled into one, as opposed to Brutus, who was all curse.

"I see a race," she said, still in her distant voice, the one he presumed was coming from somewhere else.

"A horse race or a human race?" he asked, knowing there would be no specific answer. But she surprised him.

"A horse race, a very important one."

"Oh good, something we can bet on? We are next to broke you know, running for your life because leech lovers want to kill you tends to mean you leave most everything of value behind." Rufus commented, dryly, knowing the sarcasm would simply go straight past her.

And just as he said this, Meridius sees a sign. No, not an omen, there is an ACTUAL sign about a horse race that is to be run at Woodstockium tomorrow, the town that was coming up. "There it is," cried Meridius... "the race!" Then she fell over into a dead faint, lying down beside Brutus, who was still muttering on.

Ofal beside him was also snoring away. With Meridius out cold and Brutus still waffling on in his sleep, Rufus, reliable, hard-working Rufus continued to hold the reigns of the donkey cart, as always. Well, he thought to himself, a horse race meant an opportunity for a performance which meant cash. They really needed cash! Luckily, the stage show was prepacked in the cart, otherwise, they would have had no way to make any Denarii after their rushed exit from Canadia. They would just have to go there, find whoever was putting the race on, and hope that in an out-of-the-way town like this no one would mind a leech-hating oracle and her unfunny comedians showing up.

Despite his misgivings, he was starting to feel better about having Brutus along. It was not that the fellow would defend them so much as that he just loved a good stoush. He would simply presume any people after THEM were really there to have a good fight with HIM. Well, it was coming dark, so Woodstockium was as good a place as any to pull over and camp, but as he made that decision Meridius, still unconscious, tapped him on the shoulder and with the same hand pointed to a sign to an off-road that read, "To Bethel".

Shrugging his shoulders, Rufus simply followed the pointing finger and turned down the road, whereupon he immediately met an old man with a sign saying "Bethel". Rufus is puzzled by this strange sign and stops to ask the obvious, "Are you Bethel?"

The old man looked at Rufus as if he were an idiot. "No, when a hitchhiker holds up a sign with a town's name on it, it means they are GOING to that place, in this instance, Bethel," the old man explained.

"What the hell is in Bethel?" Rufus asks.

"A Horse Race I am interested in." the old man responds.

"Isn't that at Woodstockium?" Rufus asks, now curious if there are two horse races going on.

"Yes, that is the name of the race."

"But you are going to Bethel, not Woodstockium. This makes no sense." Rufus is genuinely puzzled.

"Are you offering me a lift?" The old man raised an eyebrow, as if this was an exceedingly important question.

"It depends on what sort of political view you hold on the subject of leeches."

"I don't give a stuff about leeches. Why would anyone care about that?" the old man replies.

"Excellent, you can hop in the back, beside the crazy woman and the muttering oaf," Rufus said, glad to meet someone who had such a reasonable view on reality and leeches in particular.

Now, usually, you expect small-talk from a hitch-hiker. It is their sort of way of paying for the journey, as most would presume that picking the hitch-hiker up was because the driver of the cart was bored and wanted a person to talk to. What you don't expect is criticism. "Damn slow and exceedingly ugly horse." the old fellow says.

"That is because it is a donkey," Rufus responds.

"What in the name of Hades is a donkey?" the man asks.

"A very slow, ugly horse."

This seemed to end both the critical view on the four-legged creature pulling the cart and the conversation all in one blow. Some minutes passed, with Brutus still muttering in the background when, of all things, a RAVEN alighted on the back of the cart. It then proceeded to talk to the old man, in the 'cawing' sort of voice you would expect from a Raven. He nodded in agreement, gave the bird some morsel out of his pocket, and said, "Go back to Mars and tell him, 'Not today!' if you will."

And off the bird flies.

"Were you just chatting to a bird?" Rufus asked.

"A Raven, yes. It had a message for me."

"So you understand Raven, and the Raven understands Latin? And you just happened to meet on the back road to Bethel, on your way to a horse race? Doesn't that seem like a very large and strange sort of coincidence?" Rufus is suspecting there is more to this than meets the eye. "And you asked it to give a cryptic message to a guy named Mars?"

"Exactly." the old man agreed and said nothing more.

A dry silence ensues for a few miles, punctuated by Ofal snoring, Meridius giggling, and Brutus muttering. The sun was beginning to hang low in the sky when Rufus remembered it would be a night of the full moon, so Rufus joked, "You don't happen to be a werewolf by any chance?"

"No," the old man answers. "They were all banned to the underworld ages ago."

"I am very glad of that. Good executive decision by the Gods. I would hate to turn around on any random full moon and find the glowering red eyes of a werewolf staring at me like I was supper," Rufus jests.

"I didn't realize you spoke Raven," the old man comments.

"Why would you think I spoke Raven?" Rufus asks.

"Well, he was the one talking about werewolves."

"Oh, so I guess you then told the Raven to tell Mars, the God of War, to leave them where they were? And I suppose that, as one of the benefits of being a God being that you can talk with Ravens, this means you are a relative of Mars?" Rufus was starting to suspect he had picked up a seriously deranged nutter.

"His father, actually." the old man says. "Odd, you don't seem to be very scared. Most humans are scared when I am around."

Rufus laughs. Nutters he has no problem with. It is the sane ones who think they are the proprietors of truth and tradition, like Leech believers, who are the dangerous ones. "Well, we already have the Oracle of Delphi here, so why not toss in a few Gods. I am good with that!"

"Really?" he then looks at the sleeping woman. "Why, so you DO! Meridius, wake up darling, it's Zeus!"

Flavius Corpus

Goddamit, stooping to organizing horse races! Flavius was muttering to himself, thinking of how far he had fallen. But you had to earn a buck and out here in the sticks he was not visible to his creditors. All this because of one insane Lead Augury and a half-crazed Oracle pronouncing the End to Rome that never came. Yes, he knew it was not the same New Rome as it had been - But sacrifices were done with, which meant his position as Jupiter Optimax was now entirely ceremonial. As no more blood was being spilled that needed interpreting, and as Trumpetus Orange was buying up the Consul positions, and as creditors were baying for HIS blood, he figured the best direction for him was the exit.

Finally, people had started asking the obvious question: *Why the Hades do Gods need appeasing?* He knew why, it paid the bills. An augury a day keeps the creditors at bay, as the Etruscans always said.

No more sacrifices certainly meant bad luck for him. Now 'HE' had been made the sacrificial goat and it was all because of that damn Oracle. She had cut Flavius off from his access to the gold in the temples, plus all his gold at Delphi had been confiscated, so now, reduced to penury, he was forced into running horse races. Mind you, had he realized how profitable rigging the gambling was, he may have not bothered about all the Jupiter Optimax stuff.

The thing is, the ONE asset Flavius still possessed were his unicorns, and the one thing unicorns possessed, apart from evil tempers, was speed. They could outrun any horse, but obviously, you just had to disguise the fact of what they were. That is to say, remove the horn and dye them a dark color to hide the pink. This practice might explain, in part, their evil temperament

Powdered unicorn horn was the real reason he got them in the first place, it was worth an absolute fortune in the Far East, which was really Far West to someone in the Americas. Which was another thing that griped him, everything was still measured from Rome. Here in the new world they had bigger insulas, faster chariots, better capitalization, yet they were all still betoken to Rome. A ROMAN senator comes out and everyone is groveling in the dust trying to please him. A ROMAN horse comes out and everyone purposefully slows down to let him win.

They even sent taxes back to Rome! Of course, everyone fudged them, but this was not the point. It meant New Rome was really 'second class'

Rome. In the old country, the worst possible insult you could give a Roman was to say he belonged to New Rome. It was about damn time they booted out the old brigade entirely and started afresh. In the meantime, he had to make sure the unicorns were in a decent mood, which meant feeding them lots of sugar.

To this purpose, he had with him the very latest thing, sticks laced with a wonderful invention, spun sugar. It looked just like fairy farts but was called fairy floss. He had it dyed pink to match the natural coloring of his cantankerous creatures and the stuff worked a treat on their moods. Instead of looking at him with murder in their eyes, they put all their attention on the sugar and attacked the fairy floss with gusto. Which explained WHY he was standing there in the stalls at Bethel, waiting for the horse race, and feeding unicorns. Finally, they were full, only two wheelbarrows of the stuff and then BANG, asleep. This is what allowed him to hook up the chariot, otherwise he had absolutely no chance.

They stood there snoring as Flavius and some extremely nervous and rightfully scared staff pulled away the railings that kept them in place and slotted in a chariot. After they were strapped in, a new set of railing surrounded the whole arrangement, ready for the race on the morrow. Scary stuff this working with unicorns. Flavius checked the horn was properly filed down and filled it over with a fur patch that matched the dye. He laughed, damn he would love to take them out in their natural pink with the horn showing. People would gasp, but he would never win any money. Everyone knows there isn't a horse that can beat a unicorn.

Making sure the stalls were locked and that screens were put up to hide his secret from prying eyes, Flavius made his way back to the circus he had set up for the race. He went through all the small details: the seating arrangements, who was checked into the expensive boxes, and then making sure the rich ones were sent invites to the pre-race luncheon.

Talking to rich people was a major reason for events like this. There were so many side bets you could lay off with them without the surcharge of the bookmakers. Of course, he wore a barbarian beard and called himself 'Clithu the Gaul' in public ... Too many creditors still lurked about. But soon he would rake in enough Denarii to be able to restore his house and position in New Rome.

Flavius then went through the kitchens making sure everything was just right. He looked about, the catering tent was organized, the stalls were all in order, and all was prepared for the evening rush that would soon start. "Yes yes, Frogs Legs," he said to the caterer. "We have to have something Gaulish on the menu. And snails, you have to have more snails,"

Give the plebs plenty of food, beer, then they get all happy, and a happy Roman bets - a lot. And, of course, the favorite chariot that everyone would plunge their money on would be Master Rhodes and his famous Roman stallions. ROMAN stallions, the darlings of the masses - 'The Secretaries' they called them. (Why anyone would name a horse after a couple of slave girls, he had no idea.)

Of course, there was the small matter of the usual pre-race bribes to the stewards shop, because there was no way a dyed unicorn was going to otherwise pass muster under their careful eye. This was another reason for these out-of-town races - It was so much easier, and cheaper, to get their wax seal of approval stamped onto his unicorns chariot. Well, everything was ready. Tomorrow would bring in so much money that he was already rubbing his hands in glee at the prospect.

Of Horses and Men

Meridius opened her eyes and squealed with delight. "Daddy-boo!" she calls out and holds out her arms for a hug. The old man (who apparently was some sort of a God who just happened to be wandering through the back roads to Bethel, where there was a horse race called Woodstockium, which was miles from Bethel, was about to be held) holds out his arms, and they embrace.

"What an amazing coincidence," he says to her. "I tried to call you at Delphi, but no one picked up. Glad to see you are well my dear."

"Zeusey Baby, I am good. You heard about the ending of animal sacrifice, I gather? Is this why you are here?" Meridius was checking to see she got things right.

"Animal what?" Zeus responds, puzzled.

"Animal sacrifice, people have been killing animals and reading their entrails for thousands of years, determining the omens and portents of the Gods. I substituted a rubber chicken for a real one and it all worked fine, so we officially ended all that killing. I hope you don't mind?" Meridius was like a little girl in front of a stern father.

Zeus laughed, "Why in Hades name were people killing animals in the first place? That seems utterly ridiculous."

Rufus cannot contain himself any longer, "You didn't even know humans had been performing animal sacrifices all this time?" he asked, incredulously.

"Since when have we Gods been interested in Humans? No, what I am interested in is horses, and horse racing." Zeus responds.

"But all this talk about you seducing women..."

"Women who happened to be on HORSES, you mean? Yes, they make excellent decoration for the beasts." he chides.

"So what you are saying is we humans simply don't count for a hill of beans?" Rufus is astonished. He had always believed that his race mattered in some way, to someone, for something.

"No, not at all. I like humans because you raise excellent horses. Because of this, I make sure the sun rises and sets and the seasons go round as they should. And you need to eat, so crops, etc. all part of the Godly duties. So you see, it isn't that you don't matter, it is just that horses matter more." he explained. "Unless you are Poseidon, of course. He likes whales."

"So, all this talk about how the Gods are looking over our affairs, this is all just nonsense?" Rufus is astonished. He knew that blood sacrifice was stupid, but he believed this was because the Gods were above that sort of nonsense. Now it turns out they just didn't care.

"Well not entirely. Apollo has an interest, of sorts. I mean, he looks after the Oracles, the Oracles look after the humans, so we all pretty much considered that was our side of the job done."

"Well, your Oracle has stirred up a hornets nest about there being no need for Leeches now and it has gotten us into all sorts of bother. Can you help sort that out?" Rufus saw an opportunity.

"Oh, that was what the strange question about leeches was about? Well, not really. Strict policy of non-interference. I mean, I am happy to go on record stating I don't give a fig about Leeches, but other than that, it is entirely your business." Zeus looked upwards at the birds flying past and became entirely disinterested in anything else that Rufus had to say.

Meridius apparently had heard nothing of the prior conversation about not interfering with humans, "Zeusey sweety, can you do me the hugest biggest and most enormous favor?"

"How can I resist a cutey like you, Meridius. What would you like?"

"I have had a vision that we need to be in the Horse Race tomorrow, but we don't have any horses, or even a proper chariot. Do you think you could?"

"Anything for you my sweet," Zeus sends a bolt of lightning at some trees and from the smoke two magnificent jet black horses come forth, towing behind them an astonishing and equally black chariot, with gold and pearl inlay. One as good as any Emperors. "Will that do?"

"Perfect darling Zeusey. Just perfect. You are SUCH a peach," and she plants a huge wet kiss on his cheek.

If Rufus was astonished at the extreme degree the Gods bent the rules about non-interference, he didn't say. He presumed they could be persuaded to bend the rules if they happened to like you, but if not they became very law abiding. Regardless, he figured that win or lose tomorrow, they could cash those ponies in for a nice profit. But not before they used them to make a grand entrance into New Rome!

The donkey snorted, it suspected something was up that would make it a second class citizen. His eyes narrowed as he checked out the competition and dammit, he was sure he was seeing thing correctly - Were they WINGS he saw on those horses?

New Rome Bound

Baraka Alashad was busy organizing the details of what he was taking to New Rome when Chincino arrived back from the booking office. "You will never guess who was in the line with me?" he asked by way of a conversation his former owner did not want to have. Baraka did not guess, and naturally, silence ensued, so Chincino carried on regardless. "Focus Maximus, the Head Augury, just happens to have booked on the same boat." he lied. The fact was, he knew the African would never pass off as a slave and had insisted the Lead Augury return with them to Rome to help. "I invited him over for drinks at our cabin."

Still no response, "And I offered him three talents of gold for a good augury," still no response. "Plus free room and board for life." STILL no response. "You really aren't listening to your partner, are you?"

"We should take the gold inlay desk for the reception rooms, I think," Baraka said in an off-hand manner, in this way proving he was indeed not listening to a word his new partner had spoken.

Chincino knew this was not going to be an easy transition for Baraka, from slave owner to acting like a slave, and with his high-born attitude too many questions would be asked at customs. So he went over in front of the fellows' eyes and sat on the said desk, in order to get the mans attention. It did. "Why are you sitting on my very expensive desk?" Baraka asked.

"OUR very expensive desk, Baraka. You need to pull your head out of your arse and start thinking like a slave. If you wander into New Rome with this sort of attitude, the only thing that will happen is you get arrested and thrown into debtors prison. You aren't the first rich man that has fallen from grace and pretended to be a slave in order to get back into town. NOW, pay attention, and listen closely."

Chincino ducked the expected backhander and said, "This is precisely the sort of reaction that will get you tossed into a cave at the Tarquin, Baraka Alashad. You really need to stop thinking of yourself as an African warlord for a minute and just LISTEN!"

The man, annoyed he had missed the Greek, caught himself and muttered a sort of apology. Really though, he was only sorry that he missed, but acquiesced, "Ok, I am listening."

"We have a better plan, I met Focus Maximus on the dock, he is going back to New Rome as well and what's more, he is still classed as Head Augury. Now, despite the fact there is nothing left to augur, the position has privileges. The chief one amongst these is that he has a diplomatic passport so he goes through without too much by way of bribes, plus they will expect him to have a bodyguard. So the role you can now play is that of his bodyguard, because we have no chance passing you off as a slave. You won't need papers, because you will come in under his passport, yes?" Chincino was feeling quite pleased. The truth was that, as every hour went past, he could see how some smart customs officer was going to question their subterfuge, as Baraka had not one sniff of a slave about him.

Baraka merely nodded. "Yes, this is acceptable," he said. But then he added as an after-thought, "Does the old man understand the penalty for smuggling in a felon?"

"Of course not. He's out there in the clouds. I simply asked if he could do an old friend a favor. Despite yourself, you DID save his life, remember? Well, technically Claudius saved his life, but you gave him a safe house so he owes you." Chincino watched as the cogs ticked over. it seemed like Baraka Alashad was starting to come back to himself. The shock of losing his millions, being cast out of New Rome, which also meant all of Old Rome, and the subsequent escaping to Mexico ... it had all been a strain on both of them.

Of course, as the slave of a dispossessed owner, Chincino was also up for grabs by the creditors, so he quickly decided a life on the lam with a half-way decent fellow like Alashad was better than becoming a slave to an unknown master - So he had organized both of them out of New Rome by forging his former master, Garam Marsala's, signature. Now that his former master was a land owning Patrician and as Chincino had forged his signature a thousand times, he got the necessary visas for getting them into Mexico. He also got a good deal of the furniture and gold still in the New Rome house out of there, but Baraka was not exactly one for penny-pinching, so all the limited denarii were spent and they were still in exile.

Perhaps, somewhere deep in the recesses of the man's heart, Baraka Alashad was grateful. Perhaps. However, gratitude wasn't what Chincino needed right now. What he needed was for the man to grasp the fact he had to play a role. "Remember, you are no longer Baraka Alashad, African tribal chief, one of the richest men in the world. You are a bodyguard for a frail old man returning to his post in New Rome. Do you think you can act the part? As in, is it possible you can stop walking about and acting like you are a minor god?"

Baraka looked aggrieved. "I don't walk about like a God! Do you see gold and diamonds falling out of the nether worlds when I go past? No. If you did we would not be in this mess."

It was common knowledge that when a God walked past, having both a temporal and extemporal existence, that they shook the foundations of the physical universe and, as a consequence, things fell from other dimensions into physical reality. Most naturally presumed this would be gold and diamonds and pearls, and not horse manure and goblins, but in truth, no one really knew. The humans hadn't had Gods walking amongst them for quite some time.

This subject was a point of great discussion amongst the philosophers: Not, "Why do the Gods not walk amongst us?" but questions like: *if Poseidon swam past would he manifest gold fish? If Mars flew past, did swords and shields fall from the sky*? What, exactly, would each different God manifest? Logic said it would something aligned to what they were Gods of, but who could say? Still, you prayed to Poseidon for fish, and Mars to win a war, so the general belief was that things dropped out behind them would be in accord with the role they played.

Which raised another philosophical question: *Why hadn't anyone seen the Gods in such a long time?* It was a tremendously vexing question, one that was difficult to prove, which was possibly WHY so much animal sacrifice had been happening. People were trying to attract their attention.

One rather stupid Greek suggested that no one ever saw a God because the Gods did not give a fig about humans and that we humans were all inconsequential specks of dust in the scheme of the universe. Typical of the pessimistic Greeks, so they stoned him to death in order to stop that type of nonsense spreading. Unfortunately, this made the fellow a martyr and there was now a large following that believed firmly in the fact that the Gods did not give a rats about humans. This led to the core of their theology, which was that you therefore had to look after yourself.

The members of that particular "look after yourself" faith were generally followers of the original Sabine God of the Romans, Ops. To explain, Ops and Lucre were the two original Gods of the Latins, loosely translated as Luck and Opportunity. Every good Roman wore them as twin figurines around their necks, so despite all the many Gods and the hundreds of Temples, what the true Romans really worshipped was Luck and Opportunity.

And if you are going to have a religion, this seemed a pretty sound basis of where to start. Pray for Luck and take your opportunities! This summed up the creed of the followers of Ops. (Not to be confused with the followers of HOPS, who worshipped beer)

I mention this in passing because Chincino happened to be one of those followers and it gives you an understanding of why he sighed so deeply when he realized his sarcasm abut the Gods walking amongst us had gone entirely over Baraka's head. But regardless, as the fellow was now talking and paying some attention to the plan, he needed to keep him talking.

What better way than comparing the fellow to a God? "Well, about the God thing - they DID say you had the Midas Touch and that everything you went past turned to gold, if you remember?

"Yes, I remember. I remember it only too well," Baraka murmured. And then the man had a sort of epiphany. It was true, he did once possess what seemed god-like power and ability. What was this against his present troubles? Nothing, just a speck of time passing by. Suddenly he felt the weight of his past drop. Everything he had been, dreamed of, wished for, it was all gone. He was free of it. It was as if a ray of truth illuminated his entire being!

A deep sense of peace descended on him. A calm he had not known since slaughtering all those thousands near the Pyramids in Egypt came upon him, and a deep sense of contentment filled his heart.

Baraka looked off into the distance. Out from the balcony of their apartment, the never ceasing tide! The eternal sea sent a continual display of waves breaking against the shore. The blue sky was sketched with feathers for clouds, and a soft wind cooled his brow. It was a beautiful place. Why would they want to leave here, why would they want to go back to the aggressive and dangerous world of New Rome? "Perhaps we should just stay here?" he suggested.

The birds were singing, the wind gently caressed his brow, and Baraka felt a deep urge to do absolutely nothing but sit there and enjoy the view.

Chincino had not expected this. Where had the vengeful, malicious African warlord gone? What was this sudden change of heart? More importantly: _What about all this money he was about to make_? He jumped in to repair this sudden onset of contentment. "Of course, we COULD stay here, for a few more months. We have at least till the summer season before we have to start selling off the furniture," he emphasized the pecuniary shortfall they were suffering. "And I don't think the creditors will notice when your goods hit the auction market, not down here in Mexico, surely."

This was not really getting through. He needed to hit him hard. "Otherwise, I am sure you have forgiven Claudius and Garam Marsala and won't mind at all that they sit up there in luxury on all that gold you worked for and earned over your entire life."

That got through. Alashad leaped up, "Damn them to Hades. Pack up the things, and get Focus over here. We need to battle plan this attack on New Rome!"

Good, finally the old warlord had woken up. Depression is a terrible thing, especially when it is disguised as contentment, but there is nothing like a good fight to clear the air. Chincino was under no illusions, they were walking into a lions den.

Which reminded him, "Ah, we really can't take the lions onboard without attracting too much attention."

"What!" exclaimed Baraka. "Leave the pets behind? Who will feed them?"

"I suspect they will find someone to eat, but I have arranged for a good home for them until we are in a position to get everything sorted." Chincino was rather pleased there was no room on board, as those damn lions always seemed to be looking at him as lunch.

"An African tribal chief without pet lions is no tribal chief at all!" he protested.

"Persactly, you are NOT a tribal chief, you are a bodyguard, remember?"

"Ah, yes, I forgot. Very well then." And Baraka went back to gazing soulfully out at the ocean as he scratched his pets under the ears.

Olympus

U p in the heady heights of Mount Olympus, Mars got the Raven. "Not today" ... What the? He is confused by the terse and unexplanatory nature of the communication. He turns around to Diana and says exactly what he was thinking, "What the?" and subsequently asks the Raven to repeat the cryptic comment. It does, and in perfect classic Raven to boot. The interpreter goes over the caws to make sure they are clear, then nods to Mars that this is precisely what Zeus asked the Raven to convey.

Diana snorts, saying "Well, what day DO we start the hunt, then?"

They both were bored and wanted a bit of sport and what better sport could there be other than hunting werewolves? It was what they liked best. There was nothing like taking up your shield and spear and fighting it out with a mindless creature that only exists to eat you. The truth was, they had been terribly scarce for the last few centuries, and all because the favorite food of the werewolf was Horse. You see, Zeus had a soft spot for horses, so he had locked all the werewolves up in Hades.

Well, Uncle Hades was getting mightily sick of them. They never used a urinal, crapped wherever they pleased, and there was no way you could have a decent conversation with any of them. They were all "Arrgghh argghh I want to eat you!" AND it was coming up to full moon. Hades was now insisting they had to be put somewhere else. But where? That was when they had decided on the hunt. Let them loose on some planet, then hunt them all down. BRILLIANT! Everyone has a great time, apart from the werewolves, and the problem is solved.

It was the adventure everyone wanted. Diana was in, Mars was interested, a few of the other demi-Gods also wanted to come along - they even had some unicorns lined up to mix in some spice. The one thing a unicorn hated most, apart from everyone and everything else they hated, was a werewolf. It was always so much fun using unicorns! The stupid werewolves were so dumb as to think a unicorn was as defenseless as a horse, and they always ran right onto their horn. So a few unicorns here and there made excellent bait to draw werewolves in.

What? I just caught your passing thought and it is absolutely and completely wrong - Did you imagine for one second there that the Gods would actually RIDE unicorns in some way? Categorically not!

Dear reader, no one is that stupid. These creatures are the most cantankerous and downright nasty beasts in existence. Their preference, should you attempt such a foolish endeavor as hopping onto their back, would be to toss you up, stab you with their horn, then trample you to death. After this they may be happy for a while, as killing things has much the same effect on unicorns as eating bags of sugar. Just like fat human children, a unicorn simply cannot resist sugar, and for a time they become placid and almost friendly when enough is applied.

As a side note: The only reason Unicorns are so rare is because they have much the same egregious attitude towards each other as they do to everything else. The philosopher would argue that, on this point, the unicorn was at least they being fair. They may hate you, but they hate everyone equally. Except for werewolves - They hate werewolves even more.

And any Pegasus that crosses their path gets a good stabbing as well. They really hate those upstart, smarmy flying nags.

I should also add, while they mostly hate everyone equally, there is another exception or extra hate made for those insanely foolish enough to chop off their horn to pass them off as horses. People who do this are lined up for a particularly nasty fate.

This does not change the fact that Mars and Diana and a batch of other Gods were all kitted up for a chase of the hounds, but with nowhere to go. " 'Not today!' What the Hades does that mean?" Diana echoed.

The confusion was obvious. Mars had sent a Raven to say, "We are all ready for the werewolf hunt." and Zeus replied, "not today!"

"Then a low muttering is heard emerging from the ground. A nasty, slithering voice whispers, as a form begins to manifest in front of the Gods. "Diana is 100% correct! What the F'kin Hades DOES that mean?"

There before them, the ephemeral form of the God of the Underworld took shape, cursing and swearing, as he usually does. "Why the f'n Hades are these Fkn dogs still annoying Fkn Cerberus? I want them OUT OF THE POOL, you understand? OUT OF HADES!" The dripping greyness of the God of Death was never a pretty sight, but here in Olympus, the fellow looked horribly out of place. No wonder Zeus preferred to have him down in the Underworld.

Mars waves his hand, "I know, I know. You are upset, you have had the werewolves for too long. It's not MY fault! We WANT to hunt them, but Zeus sent us a Raven to say 'Not today' ... I have no idea what he means, but do YOU want to risk a lightning bolt? Maybe he meant not today - for hunting. Or he meant not today - or ever! Maybe he was just saying he wasn't going to be there today, but please go ahead. If you want to interpret what he means and risk it, be my guest.

"Did he really just mean go ahead and but that he wasn't coming today? Did he mean he wanted it to happen tomorrow? How do I know? You tell me!" Mars watched the malignant form of his uncle ripple with hatred. "And really, he is YOUR brother, Uncle Hades. It's not OUR decision."

Diana stepped in, "I say release them. If Zeus wanted them chained up he would have said 'Keep them under lock and key' or something like that. 'Not Today' seems to me to be saying, 'I am a little busy right now' - which is another way of saying, 'do whatever you like'."

"Fkn dogs. That's it, I have already decided ... They are GONE, you hear me, they are OUTTA here!" Hades made the decision for them. With this decision, he swooshed past the pair like a bleak wind and vapored all the way back to the Underworld.

Mars turned to Diana with a broad smile and said, "Well, now we HAVE to hunt them. Good old Hades, wearing the blame like this, as always. Do you think Zeus does this just to get a reaction from him?"

"Probably. Just as long as WE are not in the firing line. Uncle Hades is a lot further away for those lighting bolts to reach, and he's underground, so much better insulated. I really don't know why Zeus and Uncle always have to fight, but there you have it. I am kitted up, you ready to roll?" Diana was ever the practical one.

"Sure thing, Sis. Let's MOVE ON OUT!" Mars shouted the battle cry.

And so they thundered out of Mount Olympus, with their bright silver and gold chariots roaring along through the ethers. Finally, they were getting some action and hunting some of those damn Werewolves. "Did he happen to mention where he was releasing them?" Mars asked.

"We KNOW where he will let them go, Earth - right where Zeus has a whole lot of horses," Diana noted.

"Earth? For Gods sake, you mean we have to put up with that ashcan? It's just horrible there, only one sun, one moon, hot days, cold days. It is a misery. I am not sure this is all worth it." he replied.

Diana looked at him from her chariot. "No choice in the matter now. If we DON'T hunt them down and they eat up the horses, Zeus will be really pissed. Just ignore the barbarians that live there, what are they called? Humans? Just ignore them and get to it.'

On Earth, a huge roaring was to be heard and felt as thunder reverberated across the land. The hunt was on and the Chariots of the Gods were sniffing out the prey. Behind them, a stream of golden creatures, the host of angels, followed, singing the praises of Zeus and the Gods. Mars threw a few large objects at them to shut them up as he didn't want anyone scaring off the werewolves. "Did you see where Hades let them out?"

"Yes, I got them on my scanner. Looks like a place called Woodstockium."

Mars looked puzzled. Wooden Stocks? Stocking up on wood? Wearing wood stockings? Humans had the strangest names for places. They land near the town and ask a local farmer if he has seen any werewolves. He is somewhat in shock at the sight of the Gods coming to Earth but remembers the important part and looks behind them to see if they dropped off any gold or jewels. Nothing.

"Where the Hades is this horse race at Woodstockium?" he demanded of the farmer.

"Ah, what ... where did you say?" the old farmer clarified.

"Woodstockium!" Diana snapped back, irritated by the stupid humans.

"Oh, you mean the HORSE RACE? That is being held at Bethel, down the road a-ways."

"Why would they call a horse race Woodstockium if it wasn't being held at Woodstockium? Why wouldn't they call it Bethel?" Mars asked.

"Long story that," the old man takes a deep breath and starts up to tell the story, but clearly the Gods were in no mood to listen because they fired up the chariots ran down his house. The fellow supposed they did this because they were displeased with him in some way and not just because his house was in between them and the direction of Bethel.

"Ohh," said the luckless human farmer. "Not very nice of them."

His wife came out from the barn to see their already miserable lives shattered and in ruins. "What happened?" she asked, in shock.

"The Gods have favored us, darling."

The wife was extremely suspicious of the notion that Gods had favored them, as there were no pearls or gold left behind, just a bit of horse shyte.

But there IS a positive learning experience to be gained here! Finally one of the humans started to get the idea. The sad and simple truth was that the Gods truly do not care about people and far preferred hunting and horses over humans. Unfortunately, while the lesson to the farmer and his wife was an expansive one, it was also very expensive, as his insurance did not cover Acts of the Gods.

Foolishly, the man failed to read the fine print. When he applied to his insurance company the very stupid farmer explained the truth of what happened, instead of just saying a storm blew it down, he talked about Godly chariots. Obviously, the man from claims just sucked air in through their teeth and said, "Sorry - Can't help you. Act of the Gods!"

So the old man learned another important lesson, insurance companies care even less about their clients, and people in general, than the Gods.

Part Two: The Day of the Race

Whereupon there is great excitement as Gods, Wolves, Horses, Unicorns and Humans all arrive at a point of conflict where death and mayhem will ensure - until the day is saved by the donkey with it's stubborn insistence that it is every bit as good as a racehorse.

Werewolves

Contrary to popular belief, Werewolves do NOT physically change from human to wolf on a full moon. They are permanently large, and very ugly wolves with vaguely human faces that walk about on their hind legs. Unsurprisingly, they are dogs and thus have extremely sensitive ears, which is the true cause for the myth about all this changing business. What happens at full moon is that they get in a terrible mood because of all the howling the other werewolves feel compelled to do. Needless to say, they are far too insular and selfish to consider that THEY are also howling and thus part of the problem by setting off their brothers, but be that as it may - this is when they 'change'.

All the noise drives them crazy and they start snapping at anything that moves. I have even seen the odd one pick a fight with a tree on a full moon, purely because it was swaying too much in the breeze.

However, when not trying to kill everything in sight, they DO chat to each other and are quite civil when not howling. It is just that the full moon brings out the hound inside them. The compunction to howl incessantly is instinctual, but it is a little like fingernails on a chalkboard - the howling drives them into becoming senseless beasts. At all other times, you would class them merely as party animals. They DO love a party and a drink - As soon as any party starts up they love to dance, drink, tell lewd stories of their conquests, and generally go hang out in low-life bars. You may have a distant relative you recognize here?

The problem Hades had with the wolves, as he called them, was not the full moon - they were sent down there specifically because there WERE no full moons, just endless shades of grey. The issue Hades had was the never-ending party. The significantly greater noise of their carousing, curiously enough, did NOT set off the wolves to fighting amongst each other. No one knows why, other than perhaps it was traditional.

But carousing wolves WERE fingernails down the blackboard for Hades. It got to him and had him wishing all forms of plagues upon their souls. The doof music, the cheering, and the stupid hats - it was all SO irritating. (For some reason werewolves, when they party, like to wear hats, the more ridiculous the better.)

Thus the paradox: Poor Hades was in Hell being tortured when, by all accounts, it was HIS job to do the torturing.

Now you might believe that this is a pretty poor reason to hate someone, but I assure you, after a few thousand years of non-stop celebration you really, REALLY get to hate werewolves. It was an impost to begin with, only accepted because of the promise that one day 'soon' the Gods would have a hunt and kill them down to manageable numbers.

But, out of sight out of mind, Zeus was far more interested in his horses. This was the start of the whole business of them getting packed off to Hades in the first place, because werewolves preferred horse meat over all other food. Zeus wanted them away from his ponies, but Hades KNEW it was also because Zeus knew the wolves would get on his nerves.

But enough of the past, the Lord of Hell had finally put his foot down and ordered them all out of his place. "Party is OVER wolves, time to leave." Only, they didn't. Hades didn't quite reckon on this and realized that they now considered his house their home. What he needed was some sort of bait to lead them out of there, so he sent out some imps to find it. They came back with a horse race, at Woodstockium, on the Earthly realm. That would do nicely.

Showing them the poster, he casually asked one of the head werewolves if they were interested in going to a horse race, because through that door OVER THERE (he pointed) they would find it just happened to open in the general vicinity of the race. This worked a treat, and soon all the wolves had packed up the party to go hunting some horse meat. When the last one left, he locked and bolted the door behind them.

Finally, he could get back to tormenting souls in peace and quiet.

ooooOOOOOoooo

Meanwhile, out in the forest, a rather large pack of wolves were beginning to realise that all that drinking and partying for a thousand or more years meant they were not so steady on their paws. What they needed was a little peace and quiet, so they all curled up in the forest to sleep it off till tomorrow, the day of the horse race. Sadly for them, this was precisely the moment when the full moon broke over the horizon and so the howling started. Not just any howl, a thousands years of stored up unhowled howls broke free of any constraint.

Rufus looked up from the camp he had made for the night on the outskirts of Bethel and heard this insane ruckus, a howling, snarling and snapping of teeth in some distant woods. Ofal was awake by now and was helping to pitch the tents.

"What in Hades is THAT?" Ofal asked.

"Sounds like a dog fight," Rufus responds.

At this point, Brutus wakes up and says, "Dog fight! Fantastic, I love a good dog fight. Where is it?"

Ofal pointed over in the general direction of the snarling. Which also happened to be the same direction the magnificent new horses and chariot that Zeus had manifested were grazing. "Nice rig!" exclaimed Brutus. "Who owns THAT?"

"The old man over there gave them to Meridius for the race tomorrow," Rufus explained. He was going to say 'Zeus' and that 'the Gods manifested them' but such a thing would require a detailed explanation and right there and then he decided he didn't really like Brutus enough to be bothered.

"That old man over there? He looks a lot like Zeus," said Brutus.

Rufus looked up to the heavens, though why he did so he had no idea. The Gods weren't there, they were leaning against a tree contemplating their navel. "Yes well, it is Zeus, friend of Meridius, doing us a favor."

"Damn," said Brutus, accepting this as if Rufus had just said 'The moon is not made of cheese'. "She is certain to win with magnificent horses like that." He went over to chat to them and, surprisingly, they seemed to like him. So he sat there and talked for a good few minutes before coming back. "Yes, they tell me they are a shoo-in to win. Very nice ponies, good-natured as well."

"You can talk to horses?" asked Rufus, wondering what on earth Brutus was up to. He was actually being pleasant for a change.

"Oh yes, always have. I get on with them much better than I get on with people you know."

"I can't say I am surprised. The part that DID surprise me is that you bothered to listen to what they had to say," said Rufus, half sarcastically, half in earnest. In the whole time he had known the man, Brutus listened to nothing other than his own voice.

"Well, horses speak a whole lot of common sense, unlike people. Horse sense, I call it." Then he gets up, dusts off the sleep from his eyes, and says with enormous enthusiasm, "Right then! Dog fights mean betting and booze, so I am off! See you at the race tomorrow!" And, as the full moon crested over the horizon, he was gone in the direction of the howling.

Zeus looked up from doing whatever it was that Gods do when they are sitting and thinking. In truth, it is probably nothing at all. If it were anyone else sitting and doing nothing you would think no more of it, but when a God sits and does nothing, for some reason you just believe they are doing something important. This was, Rufus suspected, half the secret of being a God, the ability to do nothing at all - that and their powers of manifestation.

Zeus hears the snarling, sees Brutus heading off in that direction, and asks Rufus, "So where is your friend going?"

"He is not a friend, more an annoyance wanting a lift to New Rome. But he is off to the Dog Fights over in yonder woods." Rufus answers.

Zeus wanders over to the camp and, FINALLY, things start dropping out of alternative universes as he walks. Mind you, they are things like toasters and blow dryers, items of no value at all because in the particular dimension where Rufus lived, electricity had not yet been discovered. But at least there was SOME sort of manifesting starting to happen. It gets Rufus thinking. "Ah, Zeus, how come you are manifesting things behind you now, but nothing for all of the previous day?" he asks.

Zeus looks back and sees all the accoutrements of some alternative universes dropping into the present reality. "Oh, it only happens we Gods WALK on the face of the planet. Something to do with ionic interference and breaking down inter-world frequency barriers, or some such. I had Tesla explain it all to me a century or so ago. Sitting in a cart means I don't have physical contact with the ground, therefore I do not 'earth out'. At least that is how he explained it."

"I don't suppose you could walk in such a way that gold and jewels drop out of the sky?" Rufus asked, hoping beyond hope that this God might be courteous enough to oblige him.

"Nothing to do with me, young man." Zeus deferred. "Just something that happens. Whatever dimension I, or any other God, are presently bumping against gets shaken up by the energy of us walking along, and things fall through. It is one of the main reasons the old Greeks asked us to stay on Olympus."

"What?" exclaimed Rufus. "Why on earth would anyone want to stop things manifesting all over the place?"

"Well, part of the reason is where your friend is going, over to the Werewolves that are having a fight. You see, at one point I was wandering along and trolls and werewolves were dropping in. They really made a hell of a mess with their constant partying, and they really annoyed me by eating a whole lot of horses. So I sent them all off to Hades. Seems like Brother Hades finally has had enough and evicted them." Zeus explained.

If Zeus considered the next logical step, which was the heavenly horde descending from Olympus to kill the dogs, he didn't mention it.

The Party

It was a hell of a sight - brawling, shouting, drinking - and the weird way they all wore those crazy hats! It was, in short, just the sort of party Brutus loved. "Yeee haaa!" he said as he leaped into the fray, swatting and bopping and tossing bodies around. Man, these boys really knew how to have a good time.

"Arrrroooooo!" howled a wolf at the moon, with the response being that ten other wolves pouncing on him. This was another extremely unfortunate thing about wolves: They howl when excited, so the ones doing the pouncing ALSO go "AAArrrhhoooo" ... and I guess you get the general picture. It was a bun fight of epic proportions.

Brutus only saw the fun part, all these crazy dudes jumping on each other and fighting. He presumed it must be some special lodge who dressed in wolf skins. Which made it even BETTER! He really loved lodge parties, because they hammered hard. Then he realized, dammit, this party had no DJ? What this jumpfest needed was some hot funk, and right then he saw a fully set up, unattended drum kit. He headed over to it and started to beat out a rhythm. "Boom boom boom," went Brutus. "ARRRHHOOOO" went the wolves. And so the net result was a sort of cacophony of "Boom boom boom - Arrhhhopooo" What a groove! The mix of howl and doof really put the party over the edge. The wolfmen just went crazy!

However, as luck would have it for Brutus, wolf society had one fixed rule. Only one, mind you - You must not eat the musicians. Whether by some deep survival instinct, or sheer luck, (we can presume the latter) Brutus managed to slot into the one spot where he was safe. All around him the werewolves went totally fruit loops, howling, biting, savaging their own - and all the time, while the fur flew, Brutus sat there on the drums, beating away and howling along with his lodge friends.

It was a GREAT PARTY. Maybe even the best he had ever gone to. Finally, it dawned on him, he had been sitting there drumming away and had forgotten about the drinking. "Where's the booze?" he called out.

Now there is a second rule of werewolf society, but it was such a given no one had ever written it down. After not killing the musicians, the second rule is being nice to them, a thing called hospitality. A person asking for a drink called this rule into play.

Simple guidelines are what make all societies function. In this case: Don't eat the musicians, and always offer someone a drink. These are, of course, the essential principles that any civilized society should obey. So the wolves had to stop, rummage around, and find some booze. Of course, when they found the booze, they all stopped howling and forgot about their arguments, so the whole thing settled down ... Remember this if you ever end up at a werewolf party on a full moon - it is very difficult to howl when knocking down a beer.

"Yeah Baby!" shouts Brutus as he is handed his ninth beer. "You boys know how to PARTAY!" And so the drinking goes on till the early hours of the morning, with Brutus having a fantastic time and the werewolves deciding that maybe these humans weren't so bad after all.

At last, in the wee hours of the morning, he gets to talk to some of the wolves that are leaning up against him, happy and content in an alcoholic haze. "So, where you boys come from then?" he asks.

"Hades," they all reply in unison.

Brutus roars with laughter. "Damn straight!" he says. "You are my sort of boys. You here for the horse race?"

The ears prick up, and sobriety starts to set in as the sun rises and the moon fades. "Ah, yes. Do you happen to know where it is?"

"Not exactly, but we can go find it. It's over in that direction," Brutus points in the general area of where he thinks Bethel lies.

"You like horses as well?" one of the werewolves asks.

"I love the ponies," says Brutus, presuming the fellow was talking about betting. "Some of my best parties have been at horse races!"

All the wolves laugh. What a great fellow they fell in with, and such courage, walking into a ravaging horde of wolves insane with blood lust under a full moon. Just as they were looking at each other as if they had all just found a new favorite pet, the leader of the pack came over. Why? Jjust liking someone was not enough - you needed to test a newcomer, to make sure he was acceptable. "So, what would you do if I tried to bite you?"

Brutus roared with laughter. "I just love it! Love you guys, love your party, love the outfits - you're the BEST!"

At which point the pack leader launches at him, not actually intending to bite, just to see how he reacts. Well, Brutus reacts alrighty. He knows a frat party when he sees one and understands how there is always one who is testing the waters. You have to show them who's boss. So he thumps the wolf to the ground while he is in mid-flight. "Now now," he says, "You got to behave or I get mad, ok?"

Well, in wolf society, when you defeat the pack leader in a fight, which this surely was, you BECOME the pack leader. The Wolves were impressed and all nodded in approval, thinking, "Hmmm, a human has beaten one of their own in a fair fight. And he didn't even raise a sweat?"

Of course, the clan leader was drunk beyond redemption and absolutely did not expect the human to do anything but run. The fact the fellow landed a haymaker right on the top of his head, the only spot a werewolf was vulnerable, took him completely by surprise. He came to with stars in his eyes, and the view of all the wolves carrying the human on their shoulders, cheering him.

The Day of the Race

Flavius Corpus was busy. He had been kept up all night with that damn howling and carrying on in the woods, but worse than that, his unicorns were beyond crazy. He had them locked up with iron chains, but they had pulled so hard they were about to break the wood they were locked into. Damn, but they were upset over something.

He had to crank up the fairy floss machine in the middle of the night to manufacture a calming sugar hit

Finally, in the early hours, the howling stopped and they settled down, but it was a close call. If they had gotten away, there was no catching them and all the bets he had laid off onto them would have been wasted. You see, the trick with these races was to bring in a ringer that everyone thought would win. In this case, a charioteer from Old Rome had been brought over and everyone presumed he would waltz it in.

Master Rhodes, the great and famous charioteer from Old Rome, had never been beaten. HE was the ringer, the odds on favorite who was soaking up all the money from the punters

As Flavius had tame bookmakers along with him, they knew the score, and in return for the bonanza of profit they were to make with the favorite not winning, they gave him fifty to one odds on his own horses/unicorns. It was a very agreeable arrangement for all parties, with only the punters losing, as indeed the punters should. However, if he had no unicorns to race, the possibility of the favorite getting up was significant. This would cause a considerable reversal of fortunes, because not only would he lose his stake in the race, the bookies would be after his blood for their loses.

But, no risk of that. He had UNICORNS. Zeus himself could not outrun them.

The Godly Chariot

That morning saw Meridius sitting there in some distant space, but this time it was alongside Zeus, who also appeared to be nowhere in particular. As the sun rose both were just gazing out over the countryside, apparently communing with nature. The boys had packed up camp, fed the horses (who were still there, fortunately) and prepared breakfast when Rufus said, quite loudly. "We need to get into town and register the ponies for the race!" But to no effect, the pair both just sat there, zoning out.

Well, at least that Brutus was still preoccupied and had not returned to annoy him. He turned to Ofal and said, "I will take the horses in and do the registration thing, you bring this lot along in the cart when they decide to come back from wherever it is they are."

Ofal nodded, "What if they don't snap out of it? You know how Meridius can be, and we have no idea how much worse a sense of time that Zeus will have."

"Safe to say, I expect he will have no sense of time at all. It seems all these flighty out-world types live in their own time zone. I gather part of the requirement for being spiritual is to not give a stuff about schedules and being punctual." Rufus sniffed the air acrimoniously.

In his way, he adored Meridius, both he and Ofal did - but she could be difficult. However, he remained grateful, she had brought them up from low life unfunny comedians to world-famous unfunny comedians. Her not being present for large portions of time was just part of the deal. "I will see about setting up a pre-race show and organize a room for the night in town. I don't want to camp out again because I didn't like all that howling with the full moon and we got another one this evening."

But as Rufus settled the very wild horses that were still strapped in to their chariot by offering them some sugar cubes, Zeus just appeared beside him. "So, you are entering the race then?"

Covering up his surprise at the surprise, Rufus nodded. "Well, I suppose we will, given that we have race horses and a chariot and there is a race on." Rufus found his sarcasm entirely missed Zeus and instead he found himself mildly flummoxed that he was not a lot more flummoxed about chatting with a God, especially before breakfast.

"Who is the Charioteer, then?" Zeus asks with a sort of whistle in his voice, as if to say 'pick me!'.

"I was supposing it would have to be me," Rufus answered, refusing to rise to the bait.

"You have raced chariots before?" Zeus asked, nonchalantly.

"We certainly have been chased in them on occasions, a very similar situation." Rufus already had the general idea of why the the notion of non-interference was discarded with so easily. Zeus just stood there with his hands behind his back, now openly whistling. It was a less than subtle hint. "Tell me, Zeus. As a curiosity, have YOU raced Chariots before?"

"Why yes, I HAVE now that you mention it. I am told I am quite good." The God continues to whistle now adding a bit of a hum to it.

"I don't suppose part of you coming here, manifesting these magnificent beasts and hanging about has anything to do with you wanting to be IN the race, would it?" Rufus queried.

"Weeeeellll... I have to admit the thought DID cross my mind." Zeus casually mentioned.

"Fine then," Rufus said resignedly. He knew nothing was going to be straightforward about this race that Meridius dreamed up. "Shall we go into town and register you and the horses for the meet?"

"Excellent suggestion. And yes, I will do it, as you so kindly asked and as you need someone to take the reigns, so to speak." Zeus was beyond happy. A HORSE RACE, his most favorite of all his most favorite things. As he popped up he indicated for Rufus to come alongside him.

"Now the secret to Chariot racing is understanding the tricks of the trade," he said conspiratorially. "The first thing to grasp is how to employ the spinning daggers that shoot out from the hubs. Excellent for taking out the spokes of the enemy, I mean, competitor." He flips a lever, and these evil-looking swords pop out from both axels. "You can use just one, (he flips a lever and only the right-hand axel blade pops out) or the other." (With this lever the right side goes in, and the left-hand sword goes out)

Rufus looked and wondered why on earth, or not earth as the case might be, that a God needed to cheat, but he said nothing. "There are also the tintacks - you see that leather pouch at the back? It is not a tool kit, it is full of tacks designed to hurt the hooves of the horses following you. Obviously, they will have these tricks as well, so OUR ponies have extra thick shoes. That's not all, see the metal spring suspension? Latest technology, you can hit a boulder thrown off the back of an opponents chariot and you won't necessarily break a wheel."

"Wait a minute, are you saying these chariot races are basically won by those who cheat best?" Rufus was somewhat shocked.

"No, of course not. You have to put in some hefty bribes as well," Zeus seemed shocked the lad knew so little about the sport of kings, and Gods.

"It has nothing to do with who has the fastest horses?" he asked.

"Of course it does. All we are doing is HELPING them, by hindering everyone else."

"It does not exactly seem fair to me," Rufus says.

"All's fair in love and horse racing," replies Zeus.

"All's fair in love and WAR, you mean?" Rufus checks.

"Exactly what I just said," Zeus gees up the horses as they both climb in. The ponies love it! They eagerly kick up heels and are AWAY. Rufus could hardly believe the speed of these things, it made the ordinary town chariots seem more like his donkey and cart. "Now," shouted Zeus over the thundering of hooves, "Your role is very important. As the Charioteers assistant, you are expected to work the levers and throw sharp objects at the other chariots. I have a few spears, but the best intimidation is always a few arrows. Are you any good with a bow and arrow?"

"I am not much of a weapons person," admitted Rufus.

"Well, start learning. Arrows may not bother me, but they will certainly bother YOU, and you can be absolutely certain the assistants on the other machines will be targeting your sorry little arse."

The fortunate part of having a God for a chariot driver is the never-ending supply of arrows that appear in the quiver beside him. It allows for an enormous amount of practice. And so Rufus duly practiced all the way into Bethel. He managed to hit a tree once, not the one he was aiming at, but he didn't admit to that.

Perhaps it was fortunate they booked in so late and that Flavius was preoccupied calming his unicorns, because the booking clerk just took their details and entered them into the race without the usual pre-race inspection. Generally, under an experienced stewards gaze, things like wings folded neatly on the flanks of a horse would indicate that something was not quite right. But as it stood, two black horses, one black chariot, and the name of the team?

Zeus had already wandered away, this time leaving an assortment of strange musical instruments falling from the nether-worlds behind him, along with some pieces of round plastic in cardboard sleeves that said "The Rolling Stones". Rufus thought these things might be useful and, taking one of the black discs out, he threw it. Thus he invented the Frisbee.

A cough in the background brought him back, "Ah, the NAME of the team? The TEAMS NAME?" demanded the clerk.

"Nobody in particular," said Rufus.

"We need a name and, when I get a name, I issue you with a number, then the punters know who not to bet on, yes?" the clerk was insistent.

"Mount Olympus, then," snorted Rufus.

"Oh my, aren't we being humble," the clerk sneered, but entered carefully the team name as Mount Olympus. "Your number is thirteen, unlucky thirteen. Take the horses to the stable, the race starts at midday and consists of twelve laps of the circus. Winner takes all."

"Ah, and may I ask how much the prize is?" Rufus had no idea, but was hoping it would be enough to set them up for New Rome.

"Dream on Pleb. You will be lucky to see the second lap, but if you win, five gold talents." the clerk says as he walks off.

Rufus almost lost control of his bowels. FIVE Gold Talents for a HORSE RACE? You could buy a few decent country properties with Five Gold Talents. "Ah," he shouted after the clerk, "Who is the competition?"

The man turned and sneered at the lowly soul who turned up late, "Better, faster and more likely to win that you will ever be. We have one of Old Rome's leading charioteers here, Master Rhodes."

Ah! He knew that name, the posters all over the old country had him as a favorite in all the main chariot races. "All Rhodes Lead to Rome" as they used to say in the promotional pamphlets. Damn, Rhodes had never lost a race, and now Rufus remembered why. His second was a master archer and, as a result, not too many of the competition lived to finish, let alone manage to compete.

Rufus casually took out another black disc and sent it whistling through the air, watching as it arced around the corner causing someone to cry out as it struck them. "Hmmm," he started to think. "There could be something useful in these things."

The Day of the Hunt

Mars and Diana were washed and ready for the day. They had their winged chariots all prepared, with plenty of weapons tinged with silver which, as you know, is ruinous to werewolves. They look about to make sure the beaters were all fanned out in a tidy arc. Everything looked set. It was a simple business, you make a lot of noise on the perimeter, the wolves get all flustered and confused, you come in and start chopping them up. Military 101, break up the center, then hack down the fleeing soldiers, or wolves, in this case.

It would have all been so simple IF the wolves had not found themselves a new leader overnight, one who understood war and battle tactics. As it stood, they were all rudely woken out of an early morning slumber fest by a tooting of horns and a rattling of shields. The wolves started to panic, they knew a roundup if ever they heard one and were about to run for their lives. But Brutus called them all back, "What, you are running from a few horns and a rattling of swords on shields? Noooo. this is an INVITATION! This is the best sort of party you can have!" He bellowed to them all.

The fact that their new leader seemed quite excited by the prospect of being hunted down caused the werewolves to stop and pause. Was he mad? But Brutus was laughing, "Friends, (he didn't quite realize they were werewolves yet, he was not very smart) this is an old trick ... Don't panic. Form up lines, grab some weapons. This is the MOST FUN you will ever have, it is called WAR. This is what I do best, and a good fight is what we all love, yes?"

Surprisingly, this made sense to the wolves. They gathered round, and listened to their new human leader and started to feel that maybe there was some sort of portent in this strange circumstance. After all, if he fails, they can eat him. It's a sort of win/win. But there was a problem. "Arrhhoooo." one of them asks.

Now, you must understand, at this point Brutus had no idea he was a Demi-God, or that one of the unique abilities of such a being is the ability to understand animals when they speak. To HIM it was no curious howl at all, it was a simple question. This question was, "How do we pick up weapons, we only have paws?"

Now that the morning light is making things clearer, it is finally dawning on Brutus that his friends from the night before were, in fact, werewolves. Well, it doesn't pay to judge another by their looks. Accept reality, move with the flow, and all of that. "Do you have rope?" he asks.

"Owww rrr ow." answer one, which was, "Of course we have rope. We use it to tie the booze to the wagons."

"Great," says Brutus, what we need do is work in packs, you guys should be good at that, yes? (they nod) Well, grab some rope between the teeth, and run directly in line behind each other through the woods. Make sure you don't wrap each other round a tree. Now, when you find the opposition, run right at them, then split in two as you come up. The rope will stretch tight, which will trip them over, and you can have at it." It was a simple plan, but better than running away.

So instead of a pack of confused wolves running all over and being easy pickings, what the heavenly hunting party found was set of wolves running AT them, despite the noise, and tripping up all the retainers, and setting onto them. Sure, when Mars or Diana wheeled around to take them on, they took off, but then they turned back and came in from behind to set onto more retainers. After just twenty minutes of this, they were running low on staff. "Back off," called out Mars. And they all pulled back to regroup and work out a new strategy.

The wolves cheered their new leader. This was the first time they had ever beaten the Gods in battle and they were feeling pretty chuffed with themselves. They came back to camp to lick their wounds, literally, and realizing the day had moved on - it was already time to think of getting to the horse race. "I can't believe you guys love horse racing as well!" cried Brutus, utterly delighted with his new-found friends and the days business.

"Oh, we love horses alrighty," said the wolves, salivating at the thought.

000ooo000ooo000

Mars rounded up the troops and started abusing them, "You lot got routed by a pack of WOLVES. Do you know how HUMILIATING this is? We will be the LAUGHING STOCK of all Olympus." Then Diana eased in and used feminine wiles to settle the situation.

"To be fair, they did something new and were organized. Somehow they knew what we were doing, and developed a way to counter it. This is a bit of a first. But we know why they are here!" She holds up a leaflet for the horse race. "We know they can't resist horse flesh, so all we have to do is wait near the race and it is a certainty they will turn up midway and try and catch some of the runners. So, for now we let them think they have won. They will relax and go after the horses. When they jump onto the track, our archers will pick them off.

"Now Mars darling," she continued, "we need to get ourselves into that race. One, to make sure Zeus isn't interfered with, and two because it will be so much fun. Further, the wolves will be so full of bloodlust they won't recognize us. That means we will have the best hunting right in the middle of the fray, what do you say?"

Mars nods his approval, "A good plan, no wonder you are such a good huntress. We will go in and enter the race. All you men, take your bows and swords, and make sure you find good vantage points in and around the stadium. Wait for my signal, but if you can't see me for any reason, as soon as the wolves start jumping onto the track, take that as the time to start firing."

000ooo000ooo000

The clerk of the course blinked, twice. TWO more entries and TWO incredible horses teams with TWO more magnificent chariots that had astoundingly rich royals driving them? Who would have thought a little out of the way horse race would draw so much attention. This is going to drive the bookmakers nuts, but he points them towards the stables and says the race starts in two hours.

Of course, all these new competitors were the talk of the race, and people started to line up outside the stabling area to catch a glimpse of the newcomers. Up to that point, everyone thought it was a given that Master Rhodes would win. All New Rome leads to Rhodes, they quipped. Now people were not so certain. True, these newcomers had no track record, no history to speak of, but the horses and the chariots were truly a sight to behold. It was like the Gods themselves had come to earth, they were so astonishingly beautiful.

Of course, as soon as Mars and Diana entered, they saw Zeus' rig parked up and ready to race. "Of course! This is why he didn't want the wolves about!" exclaimed Mars, getting the idea at last. "He didn't want them interfering with his race."

"Have you considered that he won't want US interfering with his race?" Dianna commented dryly.

"We aren't here to win, but to kill the wolves," Mars replied. "Zeus will be very pleased we are here to help him out. But this is interesting, obviously some of the humans have gotten smart." he indicated over to the back of the stalls. "I swear those are UNICORNS I see over there - died black, with the horns off, but they have that same evil temperament. I would recognize them anywhere."

Diana peers over, "I believe you are correct dear brother, that really puts the cat amongst the pigeons, or Pegasus amongst the Unicorns to be precise. Unicorns hate wolves, don't they?"

"Even more than people," laughs Mars. "Look, they are getting itchy ... seems to me they already have wind of them." He goes over to the stable the two sets of unicorns are being held in. They kick their heels and get annoyed. This is not just because they are always irritated but from their irrational hatred of Olympic Gods. You see, in the distant past, a terrible thing happened to make unicorns hate the Pegasus and the Gods.

It is a little known fact, but right at the start of the God business, one of the priorities was choosing who or what would pull their chariots. Much was made of the entire business, but in a nutshell, after much consideration the Pegasus were chosen to pull the heavenly chariots over the unicorns. The Unicorns were mightily pissed off, muttering as they left the selection field, "So what if they can fly, they got no horn!"

Some would say this was the start of their incredibly bad temper, but I suspect it was there all along and that they were only acting nice because they wanted 'in' on the whole Olympus thing. However, what IS certain is that unicorns now take a particular exception to Gods and flying horses.

Diana was just behind Mars, laughing. "You know those unicorns are going to go us, don't you? They won't give two hoots about the race. Their only choice will between who will be first - us in the ring, or the wolves."

"No horn, that will frustrate them even more!" Mars laughs loudly. "They will be so angry and when the wolves turn up? HA! We know what happens then: Mayhem. This is going to be so much fun. Absolute madness and Daddy will be sooooo pissed we spoiled his race." Mars is beside himself with mirth, thus aggravating the unicorns even more.

Diana was far cooler. "You laugh now, but what about when he loses his cool and the lighting bolts start to fly? It might be at the wolves, at the unicorns, or it might be at US! Once he lets go who knows where or when it will stop. We both have seen how he gets when he gets his dander up."

Mars nodded. "Yeah, but he also loves a good race and though he won't admit it, he will love the fact we are here making a real show of it. Right now I expect he will be in the bar drinking, and happy, so let's not interrupt him until the very last moment. It will be a surprise and if he goes really OTT (over the top) we can always fly off."

"Not concerned about the spectators or our own people being eaten by wolves, or anything like that?" Diana queries.

Mars scoffs, "Sure, deeply concerned. Make a note of it."

TIME

Rufus stabled the horses and gave them some treats. It appeared they decided he was ok, because they neither bit nor kicked him. This was unlike what they did to the stable boy who turned up and said something about 'wings' and 'foul tempered horses' to them directly. He was booted out the stable door and now lay there unconscious, possibly dead. Still, the good lad had left all that tasty Lucerne behind, which the Pegasus loved.

Thus Rufus had found them in reasonable spirits, chomping away. He started patting them down, chatting away at how excellent they looked, and how much they would be worth in the auction rooms of New Rome, when he suddenly realized he hadn't eaten himself.

So excusing himself, he went off to find some carnival food and a bar to wash it down. Of course, right there in the first bar he walks into, Zeus is regaling the plebs with the stories of his great endeavors. In between chatting about how great he is, he quaffs down an ale, and then another. Then another, and then a few more. Rufus figured the God had made a sizable dent in the keg already.

Zeus was off and discoursing on the greatness of the universe, when someone happens to ask, "What time is the race?" Well, didn't THAT set him off!

"Time? You talk about TIME? You fools, why are you trapped by TIME? It is a bendable instrument, a tool of the Gods. We use time to manifest worlds, it is sundial of moments that we gather together to form a new reality. The race occurs at the time appointed not by MAN, but by the GODS!" he roared, apparently very satisfied that this answered the fellows' question.

Rufus interpreted, "He means noon, two hours from now." After which he asked for a lager, without flies - which was extra, but worth it. Tossing a few Denarii on the counter, he goes to sit over by a tent flap to watch the passing parade, when he heard the now familiar roar of Zeus coming up behind him.

"I like these people," he said. "Not as much as horses, of course, but they are OK. How are our little friends doing?"

"I gave them some sugar, they found some Lucerne after beating a stable boy half to death. Overall they are happy and I swear they are excited as all Hades to be having a race. Smart creatures, horses."

"Horses? HO, better not let them hear you call them THAT!. They are my favorites, you know, and they love my personal chariot. They are well used to running through the heavens with it."

"Horses that run through the heavens?" Rufus was finally realized things may not be as they seem.

"Technically, a pair of Pegasus like those two beauties can't be called horses. Did you know I modeled your human horses on them? Obvious, with the variation that horses can't fly. Why did I not allow horses to fly, you ask? (Rufus didn't) Because I didn't want some smart aleck like your friend Heracles coming up to annoy us on Mount Olympus." Zeus downed yet another pint of lager.

"So, correct me if I am wrong, but what you are saying is that we are not only cheating with spikes and arrows and spears, but that we also have god-like flying creatures that look like horses. It's all perhaps just a tad unfair, don't you think?" Rufus had a sudden and strange affliction of conscience.

"Pfft," snorted Zeus. "I told you, when everyone cheats it is no longer cheating. Majority-Minority rule, if the majority are doing it, it is the rule. NOT cheating would be the stupid thing to do, especially as we are racing Unicorns."

Beer froth splattered all over Rufus' face and he snorted into his lager. "What!" he said... "Unicorns! We are racing UNICORNS?"

Ears pricked up from around the bar, Zeus put a finger to his lips and waved Rufus to silence. "Now now, you are breaking one of the basic laws of racing, *'don't tell the punters anything'*. Of course we are up against Unicorns. How else do you imagine Master Rhodes won all those races, with ORDINARY horses? Not at all, and Flavius Corpus also has a pair. They will give us some real competition because, obviously, we can't fly as that would disqualify us."

Flavius Corpus? *You don't suppose*, Rufus thinks, then puts it out of mind. That would be crazy, the Jupiter Optimax up here in no-where-land racing horses, or unicorns, rather. "Seriously, how many other people are racing unicorns?" Rufus was now thinking of all that money he had lost at race tracks.

"Quite a few," Zeus said with a wink as he drained down yet another lager. "But tell me, did you ever wonder WHY they were so fast?"

"No," said Rufus, knowing he was about to get an explanation anyway.

"Unicorns can slip through TIME," the God explained. "That is their whole trick, they appear to be running out on the track, but what they are really doing is dragging the track underneath them, staying in the same place while they alter the time and space continuum around them."

"That is a whole lot of very big words in a small sentence," said Rufus, who had absolutely no idea what Zeus was talking about.

"Unicorns are so fast because they don't actually go anywhere," Zeus explained. "They put themselves at different points in time, and do so in such a way that it appears they are running very quickly. They step out of THIS moment and into the next one several yards ahead of where they were. Technically, they could finish the race before it began, but no one would believe it, so they have to break it all down into small segments of time to make it appear they are running around the track."

Rufus just nodded as if he understood everything that was said, then asked, "Well, how can we beat them?"

"Excellent and intelligent question. Really, you are almost as smart as a horse, young man. Let me show you how it works," and with this Zeus takes a stack of bar coasters and manifests on each one a picture of some unicorns racing a couple of Pegasus, each one showing a different pose as they galloped. "Now if I show you these images individually, you say 'nice drawing,' don't you?"

Rufus took the queue, and said "Hey, nice drawing!"

"Why, thank you," said Zeus, in a courteous reply. "But when I ruffle them through at a speed, it looks like they are racing each other, yes?"

Rufus was astonished. As Zeus ruffles through the coasters, it looked as if he were watching a race unfold. "Oh, that is way cool!" the pleb exclaims.

"Yes it is, I call it a 'movie' because everything is moving. The trick is, we EDIT the movie. No matter what the unicorns do, no matter how many little time frames they jump, just like a picture on each coaster, we can draw ourselves in just ahead of them. You see, a Pegasus horse lives OUTSIDE of time, just like we Gods do. You see me here, but what you see is only a small portion of my entire being. If I were to put my ENTIRE presence into this point in space and time, I would push every other reality to the side and you would all be squashed off into some tiny corner of the universe."

Zeus loved this bit, "And so, I match my energy in space and time, the Pegasus match THEIR energy in space and time, and we do so at a point just ahead of the Unicorns. Thus we WIN!"

"Sounds more like a physics lesson than a horse race." says Rufus, feeling tiny and insignificant and not even knowing what physics was.

"Excellent!"Zeus roars in delight. "You understand perfectly! I can see that we will get on fabulously. It is very fortunate you are a Demi-God, you know. Ordinary humans can't survive in a Gods Chariot."

"WHAT!" exclaimed Rufus. "Who the Hades reckoned I was a Demi-God?"

"Don't blame me, it is that damn Apollo, breeding all over the place. You, and that strange brother of yours who went off to party with the werewolves, are the sons of Apollo."

"My BROTHER!" Rufus was aghast, he really WAS related to Brutus?

At that very moment, Meridius and Ofal turn up with the donkey cart.

He Haw, He Hamed, He Honkered

Meridius pulled up in the cart just as the clerk of the court was downing his fifth pint. He was confused and bedazzled by the pageantry of this little race meet and said to the other patrons of the bar, "Never seen the likes, never!" Even at major city meets you don't see anything like the quality they had turned up in their little back-woods race. He was so confused he presumed the donkey and cart that had just turned up were also entrants.

This was helped along by Meridius saying "We are here for the race."

"Team name?" the clerk asked.

Meridius thought he asked her what HER name was, and just replied, "I am the Oracle"

"Well THAT figures," says the clerk. "We already have Mount Olympus, the Gods of War, and the Huntress, so why not the damn oracle as well. Off you go, up there to the stables. Race in just under two hours. So, with you and your donkey, this makes sixteen runners, which means I will make you number twenty, about where you will place."

"I like twenty," said Meridius to Ofal. "It's a good number." and looking at the stickers with the number twenty (xx) on them she added, "And what do we do with these? Never mind, I see Zeus' chariot, and, oh look, Diana and Mars are here as well. How sweet!"

The clerk just shook his head, then went back for more beer, seeking out an increased level of oblivion.

Ofal was so busy encouraging his increasingly stubborn donkey along that he really did not pay any attention to Meridius, or the clerk, other than to go where she pointed. The lad lived pretty much in his own world. Even when they pulled in and stabled the donkey (something the donkey rather liked because he usually just camped out in a field) even then he did not pay attention to what was around him. What HE was thinking of was whether Rufus had organized a performance before the race.

So he trotted off to find him, which meant looking in the bars.

In the meantime, Meridius popped over to say hello to Mars and Diana. "Hello darlings!" She called. "How sweet of you to come. What on earth brings you to earth?"

"Oh, Meridius." Diana turns and kisses her on both cheeks. (Mars nods, and winks while he stares at her tits) "So nice to see you and so unexpected. Have you seen Daddy-boos?"

"Yes, we picked him up last night. He's here for the horse race!"

"Yes, we know. Ah, I think perhaps I had better warn you, the reason WE are here is because the race is going to be invaded by werewolves."

"OOooowww," Meridius sucks air in through her teeth. "Zeusey baby won't like that."

"Neither will the unicorns," laughed Mars. "But I see you and your, er, donkey have a race number. Have YOU entered as well?"

"Is that what it means? Well, no, but we rolled in and the fellow said this was our number." Meridius answered. "But UNICORNS as well?"

Diana smiled, "Well, I am fourteen, and Mars is Fifteen, so yes sweetums, you have managed to get yourself and your donkey into the race. And DOUBLE yes, unicorns."

"Really? Well, I guess it is the will of the Gods, or at least the will of the fellow who booked us in. Wolves you say, real werewolves? Do you think they will get bitey?" she asked the Gods. She did not have to ask what the unicorns would do, everyone knew how much they hated everything.

"Oh, the wolves will get bitey alrighty," said Mars. "This lot are smarter than the average werewolves as well, so I am curious what they will get up to. No matter, we have our archers in the stands and we have entered into the race as well. We will be on the ground to clean them up, so you will be in no real danger, or at least not very much."

"Do you really have to kill them, honestly? I mean, yes they like to eat horses, and snack on people, I know, but they are alright apart from that." Meridius had no desire for bloodshed. It was what started her on the whole 'no sacrificing animals' thing.

"Yeah, we do have to kill them, hun." said Diana, smiling at her sweet but soft-hearted sister. "We are on a hunt, and they are the prey, so it is kind of the reason we are here. Probably best to just keep your donkey off to the side and out of the way. He has no hope of winning, after all."

WELL! Donkeys not only have excellent hearing, they are also very sensitive. You can insult a donkey, call it names, abuse it, and it is just water off a ducks back. But try to tell them they are not as good as a horse! That really riles them up. Donkeys have their pride as well, you know. So what if they have flying horses, and unicorns. So what if he is a 'mere' donkey, he is deserving of some respect. Our dear little fellow made up his mind there and then - he promised himself that he would show them ALL up and that he would WIN this race.

He thought of the famous words of Caesar, Veni Vidi Vici: *I came I saw I conquered!* But, as he said the words out loud in his donkey voice, it came out all confused as: *He Haw, He Hamed, He Honkered*

A Meeting of Old Friends

Flavius saw Ofal walking through the crowd. "Oh dear God, not this lot again!" he exclaimed to himself. What were they here for? Had the Oracle somehow tracked him down and was going to punish him MORE? At this point, Ofal looks up and sees Flavius. By the Gods, there was nowhere to hide. The ugly little fellow waves in a friendly manner and trots over to say hello.

"Hello!" Ofal says, easily seeing through his Gaulic barbarian disguise and apparently forgetting he was part of the reason for Flavius being cursed. What OFAL remembered was Flavius being so kind as to give him pots of money and he quite liked the man.

"Ofal, isn't it?" Flavius remained courteous, but he was wondering how much time up the Tarquin you have to serve for killing a peasant.

"Yes!" Ofal is quite pleased someone remembered him. People rarely did. "Do you know who is in charge around here? I was wanting to book the troupe in for a performance."

Part of Flavius was relieved. 'By Zues,' he thought to himself. 'They are just trying to get a gig!' Outwardly he smiled, relieved there was no plot by the universe to score more points on his arse. "Well, I am sure we can arrange something, DEAR Ofal. It's a bit late for a pre-race performance, but I am thinking come the evening festivities we could slot you in."

Of course, the evening festivities generally involved a mindless mob tearing everything apart as they come to realize the fact that the race was rigged. At that point, however, Flavius and anything of value he possessed would be long gone. With a little bit of luck, the mob will tear the accursed performers, Eruptus Non-Funnius, limb from limb. Ofal, of course, just saw they were booked in for a gig and smiled. "Good, I will let Rufus know. Ah, we usually get paid in advance?"

Flavius weighed up the cost of a few coins versus the benefit of keeping the punters occupied while he made his escape and decided it was well worth it. "Certainly old friend!" and with this he dropped a few Sestertii and Denarii into the open hands of the peasant, who kept smiling, and kept holding out his hand. Flavius grunted - robbery - but dropped in a few more coins.

"Great to meet up again!" said Ofal brightly. "Lots of Chariots in the race, should be a good day! Thank you for booking Eruptus Non-Funnius!" With this, he trotted off to tell Rufus the good news, that they both could afford a beer or three.

Flavius' ears pricked up. Lots of Chariots? There were not that many an hour ago. He called over one of the dogsbodies he had hired, told him to follow Ofal, and report everything the fellow said and did. Then he went to the Clerk of the Course, to find the man completely drunk and sprawled out on the floor of his office, muttering.

"Wake up!" Flavius poured a bucket of water over his drunken clerk, at which point the fellow propped up, spluttering. "I want to see the race list," Flavius demanded.

The fellow staggers to his desk and pulls out his scroll. "Damnedest collection of chariots I ever did see," he slurs. "Sixteen chariots all up."

"Sixteen? It was supposed to be TWELVE, ten locals, the Roman and myself. How could you go stuffing everything up like this?" and he cuffed the fellow over the ears. "Show me the list." and as he read through, something told him things were not exactly going as planned.

"Who the Hades is 'Mount Olympus'? I have never heard of that team. The Gods of War, the Huntress, and 'I am the Oracle'? Who ARE these people? What HAVE you told the bookies? How on earth is this going to affect the betting?"

At this exact point, there is a cough behind him and the representative of the bookmakers, a large, heavily muscled man who used to be a Centurion before he got kicked from the army for excessive violence, said, "Yes, exactly. What is happening as all these new chariots ARE affecting the betting."

Flavius turned about nervously. "Hello Beaticus Murderus, how nice to see you," he lied. "Ah, update me on what is happening."

"The punters are not plunging all their hard-earned on the favorite anymore. Word is, you have brought in a few OTHER ringers, high-class rigs. You wouldn't be, ahhh, thinking of changing our arrangements, would you Flavius?"

"No no, not at all, of course not." Flavius needed to calm the troubled waters. "Here, have a drink!" He went over to the bar in the clerks office and pulled out a few beers. Beer always calms down violent men, he said to himself. And as Beaticus happily drained a few pints, he explained, "Never heard of or seen the new entrants. They turned up out of the blue."

"Fantastic rigs!" slurred the very drunk clerk in the background. "It is like the Gods themselves have entered our little pony race!" Which earned him a slapping down from Flavius.

"Well," Beaticus looks over his mug at the hapless Flavius, "This is precisely what I heard, that the Gods themselves have entered this race, and intend to beat the crap out of Master Rhodes. Not that we care about

THAT, but the money is starting to go onto the new people, and I am just wanting to confirm it is still organized that Rhodes will lose."

Flavius coughed. He had no idea what was happening, but explained, "I would hardly have put every Denarii I owned onto MY horse if I thought it would lose, would I? Let's be reasonable, a few people turn up from the back blocks, wanting to put themselves against this famous Roman. So they have pretty chariots and nice looking horses, so what if the punters shift the money to them. What does it matter? You know I have MY little secret..." he says this with a knowing wink.

Yes, all the bookmakers knew he had unicorns. This was the reason why they had come to their arrangements. But Bookies don't get rich hoping things will turn out OK. "Maybe so, but I think we need to do a little fixing, to make sure none of those new ponies get up, if you know what I mean?"

"Of course, dearest Beaticus. As good as done. I will see to it right away!" This seemed to do the trick and a relieved Flavius watched as the threat of immediate violence receded and Beaticus went back to the bookmakers camp.

Goddamn it! A simple backcountry horse race and it gets all so complicated! "How much more beer you got there?" he said to the clerk.

"A few bottles," he said.

"Here (he hands him some coin) go to the tavern and buy me two kegs, untapped, and get them here quick smart." Flavius has a plan to guarantee success. It was the oldest trick, soak the hay in beer just before a race, and the horses go loopy.

Wolf Plans

Whatever Brutus thought of his new role in life, we can't be certain. He was happy because he was going to the races, where he could gamble and drink all day and the fact that he was taking a pack of werewolves with him did not seem to affect his view of the day at all. They were excellent chaps who liked to party and fight. What more could you ask for?

"Now, these races always start around noon," he said. "Are you guys going to lay some bets with me, or shall we meet in the bar?"

"What is a 'bet'?" asked one of the wolves.

"Where have YOU guys been? You can bet on these horses, as in, you put some money on the one you think will win, and if it wins, you get much more money back than you put down, unless you bet on the favorite, which pays not so much."

The wolves ears pricked up. "Did you say that betting on horses pays money? As in, money to get more booze and have a better DJ at the parties?"

"Absolutely," smiled Brutus. The thought of him not winning never crossed his mind, despite the fact he never won anything.

"How do we do this betting thing?" The pack was starting to gather round and were very interested.

"Well, first we need a few Denarii to kick-start us, but we can also provide collateral, like a firstborn son, or something like that. Then we can make bigger bets and make more money," Brutus explained.

"What if we bet on a horse, and it dies, for whatever reason?" asked one hungry wolf.

"Well, then you LOSE your money, so never bet on a sick horse." Brutus thought that was an odd question, but he was happy to answer. "Mind you, if the horse WAS sick you would get very good odds."

"What are 'odds'?"

"Exactly, this is ALWAYS the question to ask the Bookmaker, that is the person who takes you bet. You see, he looks at all the horses, and he figures out the ones that have the best or worst chance of winning. If a horse was sick, for example, it would have very little chance of winning, so it would get what we call LONG odds. That is you could get a hundred to one. This means, for every Denarii you bet, the bookmaker will give you ONE HUNDRED Denarii if that horse wins."

"So," says another, catching the general idea of where this was going. "If we all put our money on the horse that is sure not to win, but all the OTHER horses die during the race, we will make a lot of money."

"You will make a killing, as they say!" said Brutus laughing. He loved his new friends.

"Exactly!" said the wolves, in unison.

Obviously, these were smart wolves. They figured if they put all the money on the horse sure to lose and they ate every other one, their parties were sorted for months. They were liking this new leader more and more.

"Well then, lads, let's get to the course, and start having some FUN!" cried Brutus. And off they went, howling (quietly) with delight. Of course, being out and about during the day was not their normal thing and some started to feel quite sleepy. "Be with you in a minute," one would say, then another, and another, until it was only Brutus left awake and hiking into town.

He figured they would catch up after they had a few winks. Then he remembered Rufus and wasn't it Zeus he was with? They had a horse or two as he recalled, some pretty damn fine ones. He should bet on that chariot.

The Dock of New Rome

Chincino, as a certified free slave with Roman citizenship, did not have to pass through customs like everyone else. Just a small bribe was sufficient for him to get his goods off the wharf and another to make sure Focus Maximus and his 'bodyguard' were treated well. Technically, of course, Focus WAS Roman, but as a Lead Augury, he really needed to claim Etruscan heritage. It was a permissible tribe, but not Roman, so despite the fact that everyone knew him, customs still went through his bags looking for valuables to 'tax'.

As a recently former slave, Chincino was up with how it all worked, however, and carried anything of worth in nailed and sealed boxes he had personally freighted in. Not that the Augur had anything of worth, but Baraka did. As a result, he needed very little cash to bribe Baraka and Focus through safely, and soon the trio were happily ensconced in a local bar, talking about their next step.

"I suppose I could go back to reading the signs," said Focus, "but the whole business is rather messed up, with all the amateurs cutting prices as they are. I am not sure it is worth it."

"Pity you can't read the future of the stock market," said Baraka. "That is something people would pay you LOTS for."

DING! A light goes on in Chincino's head. "Of course," he said, "Brilliant idea! This could be the new business of prediction, the future of stocks and bonds. We have the Lead Augury, a tried and proven predictor of future trends. Why don't we set up in business reading the signs of where the stock market will go? We could start a whole new trend, where people can lay bets on if it is going up or down, and on what individual stocks will do ."

Baraka scratched his chin. Interesting. "But what do we use to MAKE the augury? We need some sort of ritual, and I am not sure there is one."

Focus chirped in, "Well, I used to think that, but after the rubber chicken episode, my eyes were open. You can predict the future on just about ANY sort of sign or portent. I mean, I can ask a question as to whether a particular stock will go up or down. I take any gold coin, bite it to make sure it is pure gold, then I can flip it. Caesar's head is a yes, the other side is a no. Quite simple really."

Chincino listened closely. "Yes, but we can't 'sell' the idea of a coin flip. If people made decisions based on a coin toss, they don't need US to help them. We need to give it a much better look, I mean what God is in charge of coins?"

"Moneta," they both say in response. Then Baraka explains, "The word money comes from Temple of Moneta, mostly because the Jupiter Optimax would take the gold and silver from there to make coins."

"Well, there you have it. We are in direct counsel with the Goddess Moneta and SHE is deciding where the future lies. Perfectly honest, sounds scientific, and the punters will buy it." Chincino says.

"Yes, BUT," says Baraka. "It really IS a coin flip. We are going to be right only 50% of the time, that's just common sense."

"Then we make sure it is NOT 'just a coin flip' ... What we do is that when Focus here makes a prediction, we make sure it works. Because of who and what he is, people will pay attention and start buying the stock he recommends. Only WE have the information first, so we do an early buy. As the stock goes up, we sell it off . We make a motza and ALSO prove the market predictions are correct. We can justifiably say his predictions are 100% accurate.

"This means the NEXT prediction will be treated as a hot item. People will want to get in EARLIER this time, so they will throw money at the stocks, the price will soar and then we sell out, making another fortune. This is GOLD, and I mean, literally GOLD." Chincino is very excited.

"But is it HONEST?" Focus asks, considering the moral implications.

Baraka looks at Chincino, Chincino looks at Baraka, and they both look at Focus, who looks back at them. Chincino smiles his best crocodile smile and says, "Oh, 100% absolutely guaranteed HONEST as the day is long." Baraka notices Chincino is holding his hand behind his back and crossing his fingers, in order to nullify the lie.

"Well," says Focus, "As long as it is honest, I am IN!"

"Excellent," smiles Baraka. "Now all we need is a NAME for this little operation and a way to describe the business in a sentence."

I have the perfect name," says Chincino. "You always bite the coin before flipping it, so we call it BITCOIN!"

"Got a snappy ring to it," says Baraka. "How about: *BITCOIN. We make your future GOLDEN!*"

"Not bad," says Chincino, "but maybe: *BITCOIN. Your Golden Future*"

"Love it," says Baraka, "BITCOIN. Your Golden Future. Deep Market analysis! Proven and uncompromising excellence that makes you rich!"

Focus just sat there, gazing off into space. It was quite nice to be back in New Rome again and not having everyone wanting you dead. For some reason, he started to wonder what had happened to his nephew, the one he sent off to find the Mountain of Gold. What was his name, oh yes, Brutus. He remembered now, the prophecy was that he would find GOLD in the Valley of the Wolf, which was up North somewhere.

HOT TIP

D o you call it Fate, or Destiny? On that very day, an important event emerged that changed the entire course of this story. One of Lord Rupus' journalists happened to be a bit of a horse nut and had found the perfect excuse for a fully funded out-of-town holiday. He was covering the race at Bethel and went to peek into the stables and, of course, with his trained journalistic eye, he spotted it right away. The story of the WEEK! Someone had entered a DONKEY into a horse race! Such a piece of fantastic news was certain to get front page in entertainment.

So he bribed his way in to get a closer look and an interview, if possible. This was when he noticed something odd. One of the horses of the visiting Roman, who was the mad favorite, had a bit of dye running down its leg. Dye? Was the horse getting old and needed the greys washed out? It bore closer inspection and so, with a few bottles of beer in hand, he wandered up to the guards around the perimeter of the stable, where the chariots and horses were kept.

"Brilliant setup, isn't it?" he said by way of small talk.

The guards just grunted, accepting the beer, and gave him a nod as if to say, "What do you want?"

"Erik Britain, New Rome Times lads. Just here covering the race, seeing if there is any interesting gossip." He kept up his smile while all the time looking over their shoulders to check out the horses. Dammit? Was that a patch of fur on the forehead? Could it be possible? The dye had definitely run on one section where a leg had rubbed up against a stock, and sure enough, a glimmer of pink. He had seen enough, he needed some heavy hitters in here.

He raced off to the local Raven House and booked an emergency Falcon to Lord Rupus, reverse charge, of course. Lord Rupus had a very inconvenient habit of forgetting little details like paying his journalists expenses. *"Roman Charioteer Master Rhodes using UNICORNS in race at Bethel upstate NY STOP Need backup funds and more people in the field to bribe more stable hands to get the story STOP Also, someone has entered a DONKEY into the big horse race this afternoon. STOP URGENT STOP"*

Manhattan was one hundred miles away. The high-speed bird at one hundred miles an hour would take one hour, that left barely one hour for someone to get here. Impossible. The story of the year and he didn't have enough for bribes. It was so frustrating. Erik made an executive decision -

He booked a local artist and went back in to get the story as best he could. Without enough on him to buy the story the honest way, he would have to employ deceit, lying and obfuscation. In short, everything he had learned at Journalist School was now going to be tested.

The first subterfuge would be how he would pretend he was doing what he initially thought was the real story, the donkey in the horse race. So he trots up with his artist, to find a group of people, two of them exceedingly well dressed, nattering beside the donkey stall. He walked up just as Mars had been advising Meridius about staying out of the way of the wolves."Hello!" Erik says in his brightest I-am-really-friendly-and -will-never-paint-you-as-an-evil-basket voice.

Mars just looks at him, Diana rolls her eyes, and Meridius says, "Hello," with her usual cheery voice.

"Erik Britain, New Rome Times, covering this extraordinary event. I saw your entry, a DONKEY in a horse race. I just love it and I am sure our readers would want to know why on earth you are doing it. Practical joke maybe?" He said with his smiliest voice, indicating for the artist to paint the scene. But when he looked back to check the fellow was doing his job, he discovered his artist prostrate on the ground, begging for mercy.

"Meeeerrrcy!" howled the artist. "Meeerrrcy!"

"What is he begging for?" asked Diana. "Mercury? He's not here you idiot."

"No my lady, MERCY, I am begging for MERCY!" cried the artist, who after painting Gods for so long knew exactly who was in front of him... or more correctly, standing over him.

"What good would mercy do you? You can't eat it, spend it, or do anything with it. It is an utterly useless thing to beg for. Most people are much smarter and ask for jewels, or gold, something of value. And PLEASE get up off the ground, you look like a cowpat." Diana orders. Then she turns to her brother, "You see Mars darling, these humans are positively stupid. Begging for mercy! He could ask for anything, but all he asks for is an entirely useless thing, and further, something neither of us possess. Unbelievable."

Now, by this time Erik was wondering if he was being set up. "Great joke guys, really funny. I love it. But seriously, a donkey in a horse race?" The two Gods looked at each other and just shook their heads. No wonder they never spent time in this crapholio dimension.

The artist was nervously getting back onto his feet, asking, "Er, would it be alright if I painted you all? I mean, Mars, Diana and the Oracle all together, like WOW!"

Mars just nodded, the fellow was suitably subservient and so a portrait was acceptable. The artist rapidly set up his oils. Mars then turned to the reporter. "I am curious, Eric Britain. Why are you here annoying us?"

"Ah, excellent question, Sir. As a reporter for the New Romes Times, it's my job to annoy people," he explained.

"Oh, well I make it MY job to send annoying reporters to Hades," and with this comment, Mars started sharpening his sword on a nearby whetstone.

Diana intervenes, "Now now, dear Mars. We are here for the werewolves, remember. What did you want to know, reporter person called Erik?"

The man was a fool, but he wasn't stupid. He could tell that this pair knew something was up. "I will level with you, I noticed Master Rhodes over there is using UNICORNS, not horses. I think it is a big story, and I am trying to get the scoop on it."

"I am not sure why you would want to scoop up a Unicorn, they are exceedingly dangerous. But yes, Master Rhode has unicorns, like Flavius Corpus over there as well. This is why Zeus brought along a couple of Pegasus, but the reason we brought OUR Pegasus was to kill the werewolves that will attack when the race begins." said Diana.

Erik laughed. These people were a real hoot. Comedians. "I love it, great story. Almost believed you there, but seriously, he IS using Unicorns."

Diana looked at Mars, "Are all humans this stupid?"

Mars simply grunted, "Yes." And they both went back to their chariots to wait for the race to start.

The artist had knocked out his first draft. Unbelievable, in fact, no one WOULD ever believe it. *'A painting never lies'* they say, but everyone knows they do. He would finish it off later. Meridius was looking over his shoulder as he worked and commented, "Nice use of blue."

"Thank you my Lady Oracle. Did I get your eyes right?" the artist was back to grovelling, but Meridius didn't really mind. He was a sweet boy.

"You know the Gods actually quite like artists, so stop worrying, you silly boy," she said. "And yes, you got the eyes right, but really, putting a halo behind us, it's a little over the top, don't you think?"

"Of course, my Lady, I will sort it for the final version, no halos. Do you think the Gods will approve?"

Meridius looks at him with kind eyes, and laughs, "My darling, I hope you will one day understand, the Gods really don't give a stuff about you, or anyone other than themselves. Mars and Diana will not be giving you a second thought when they are done. Unless you do something like paint them with distorted faces, like that Picasso fellow did, just to get their attention. In one minute they will never even remember you exist. A little advice: All we can do is our best, and we should do this because WE feel good doing it, not because it pleases anyone else."

Right at this point, Erik Britain is starting to recall the face in front of him. "Wait a minute," he says, rememberingly, "aren't you the Oracle of Delphi?"

"Yes sweetums, I am."

"The one that has predicted the end of Leeches?"

"Mmm," she says.

"Wow, and now you have entered your donkey into a horse race?"

"Would seem so."

"And those two patricians, the well-dressed ones, they aren't really Mars and Diana, are they. I mean, they are just dressed up as Gods for the theatre of the horse race, surely?" Erik is starting to get the picture, the whole thing was a PUBLICITY STUNT for her leech removal idea. Well enough of them using the good name of the New Rome Times for their little crusade. "Come on artist, we are out of here."

He storms out, angry and annoyed that they have toyed with him like this. They probably even painted the bit of pink dripping off the horse, to get him all excited about a great new story. It was now officially time to go to the bar and forget all about this. Unbelievable, what sort of idiot did they think he was? Unicorns, Pegasus and even WEREWOLVES thrown in for good measure. What a joke. He could see the headline he would write now, "Publicity seeking bitch in sad attempt at PR for failing concept!"

The artist leaves with him, bowing as he does so to Meridius.

Erik, of course, was so angry he completely forgot that he had sent a Falcon to the boss.

Sling Shot to Bethel

L ord Rupus received the emergency bird at a time when Trumpetus was annoying him beyond belief. The fellow had finally gone way beyond any chance of Lord Rupus putting up with another word from him, or another rally. All this guy ever did was attend rallies to say how great he was at everything and all the fools there cheered him on as if he was! But then a light from the heavens changed everything! From the foulest of foul moods, Rupus suddenly smiled. What a STORY! A DONKEY in a HORSE RACE.

Just brilliant. The nonsense about the unicorns didn't interest him, anyone into big-time horse racing knew the smart people ran unicorns and if they lived long enough to make some money from them, they deserved the cash. The trick was picking WHICH unicorns would get up, because the ordinary horses never stood a chance.

But he had to get to Bethel FAST, and the only way to do that was with a sling shot, and the only one who had one of THOSE was Trumpetus. They were both in town at yet another rally when the Falcon arrived, and the idiot, I mean, his pro-consul to be, was just walking off stage to the rapturous applause of the mob. He had to think fast.

"Trumpetus, baby... GREAT news... really GREAT news. There is a big thing happening up at Bethel that I just got wind of, big rally, loads of important people, we have to get there, but we need to be quick about it. It starts in sixty minutes."

"Hey, isn't Bethel one hundred miles away?" asked Trumpetus.

"Yeppers, we will have to take a sling shot. Let's go!" Lord Rupus drags him from the adoring masses and their need for autographs. "HUGE opportunity, big crowd, patricians by the score and it is a HORSE RACE. I know how much you love horse races."

Lord Rupus talked him all the way up to the top of Trumpetus Tower, (possibly the most garish Insula ever erected) with its huge gold letters that spelled out "Home of the Trumpinius Rex!" As they hopped into glider that would be sling shotted out of Manhattan and land, with any luck, at Bethel, Trumpetus asked, "Are they expecting us?"

"Big rally," was all Lord Rufus replied. He would sort it out later, but for now, this was the only way to get to the story, plus it was true, there were lots of people there and Trumpetus was so stupid he would believe they all came to listen to him. ""Prep the eagles!" he shouted.

Slaves to his right let loose a dozen large eagles, the lead birds that would hook up to the glider and draw it on once they got underway. Expensive business, training, feeding, maintaining a flock of eagles, but what a perfect symbol of Rome's dominance of the world and their incredible grasp on the latest and best technology.

And they were OFF! The glider was set into a huge ballista which, when fired, rocketed them up into the sky where the eagles would come in and take the lead bar, thus maintain the flight. The trick was having a live bait animal just in front of them that they would go after, a 'rabbit on a stick' as they called it.

So in no time at all, they were flying at high speed towards the horse race. Lord Rupus had found some posters which Trumpetus looked at. "It's called Woodstockium, yes?"

Rupus nodded.

"But it's at Bethel?"

Rupus nodded again.

"Doesn't make a lot of sense, does it?"

Rupus nodded, "No, but there are lots of people there. Big rally. Important votes, people who love you." Short sentences were the only thing that worked, and once spoken there was little else to say. So, in relative silence, they made their way as a great rate of knots towards a tremendous event that would soon become history.

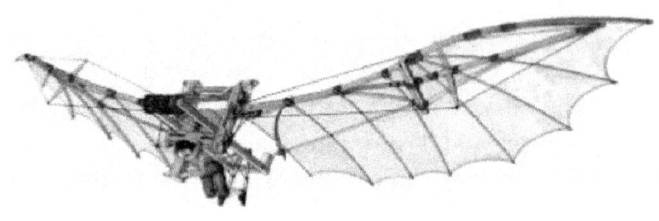

Performance Jitters

R ufus looked up at Olaf, who had found himself and Zeus in the bar, drinking happily. Then he looked at the rather large pile of coin his compatriot had extracted from, would you believe, Flavius Corpus. Who would have thought? "And you say he wants us to put on a performance this EVENING?"

"Yeah, in the evening, when everyone is happy and dunk and needing entertainment." Ofal was quite pleased with his entrepreneurial abilities.

"You realize he hates us, don't you?" Rufus noted, understanding a set-up when he sees one.

Ofal look confused, "But he gave us the gig, how could he hate us?"

"Ofal, dear Ofal, the Golden Rule, never appear AFTER the main act. And you know why?"

Ofal shakes his head in the negative.

"Because by then they are drunk and the vast majority of them have lost money on a rigged race. They are angry and nasty and ready to tear anyone who upsets them limb from limb. Are you getting the picture?"

Ofal shakes his head in the negative, again.

"They will kill us, Ofal. We will become the focus of all their agitation, and they will tear us all to tiny little pieces." Rufus concluded.

"Oh, so I have to give the money back, then?" He is very disconsolate, all his brilliant efforts have come to naught.

"Not at all, we are going on PRE-RACE. Doing a full performance, that way Flavius can make no claim to get the money back. Now, I am booked in as a second charioteer on Zeus' chariot, so you and Meridius get the donkey and cart out there and, as soon as the race starts, pack up the kit. The crowd is going to get ugly because we have Zeus as a ringer, and a lot of people will lose a lot of money, so we will be OUT of here."

"Ah, another thing," says Ofal, not knowing how this will go down.

Rufus looks displeased. He knew 'another thing' was never good.

"Meridius accidentally entered us into the race, with the donkey."

"What the? Why would Meridius do a thing like that?" It is Rufus' turn to be confused.

"I don't think she intended to," Ofal admitted.

"It's getting more complicated." Rufus was going to say more, but then he realized that Brutus had not returned from the werewolf reunion from last night. "Have you seen Brutus?" and just at that moment they heard his large, booming voice ordering a beer at the bar.

Rufus found himself strangely of two minds. Obviously, he had not yet shared his Demi-God status with anyone, but it was beginning to dawn on him that this also meant Brutus was not only his, he presumed half-brother, but that he also would ALSO be a Demi-God. This might be a tad difficult to explain. Perhaps it is best simply not to say anything? Perhaps it would be best just to turn around and walk away, pretending none of this ever happened? But before he could make his escape, Brutus clapped eyes on him, "Rufus old chap. Wonderful to see you. I made some marvelous new friends!"

"Werewolves, you mean," sighed Rufus. "How in the name of Hades did you manage to survive?"

"Marvellous chaps. They are coming here after they have slept off the evening festivities and that tremendous early morning defense we put up against all the war chariots. I am here to lay bets for them all." Brutus was all smiles, and waved to Zeus, who ignored him. "You would be the 'I am the Oracle' entry I figured, so I put everything on that - Zeus's horses are certain to win."

Now perhaps Brutus forgot, but he was in a bar surrounded by punters, who all had their ears out for the slightest tip. And what they heard was that Zeus was in the race, and that his chariot was called 'I am the Oracle'. At this exact point in time, everything went the distinct color of silence. You could have heard a pin drop, and then the people started putting two and two together ... The old man over there by the window, telling them all those incredible tales. Now they looked at their coins, and there he was, in profile, on every one of them.

By ZEUS, it WAS Zeus! They stampeded out of there to put all their money on "I am the Oracle' leaving the place strangely empty. "Ah," Ofal put up his hand to speak. "I think that was our donkey you bet on."

"Harrumph, whoever heard of a Donkey in a horse race? Who would do such a thing?" Brutus was laughing so hard, all his money on a DONKEY. What a joke. But Ofal did not correct him, or say otherwise. "What, you mean you really DID enter your DONKEY into this race, and call it 'I am the Oracle'?"

The hapless Ofal just nodded, knowing this was not going to be good. "Well, what will all my pals think when they turn up? I put everything on a damn donkey."

"Your pals?" asked Ofal, slightly miffed as he had imagined, despite the fact that no one liked Brutus, that 'they' were who were supposed to fit that category.

"Yes, my werewolf friends..."

Zeus certainly heard THAT. "Werewolves coming here!" he bellowed. "I thought Mars was supposed to be dealing with them?"

"The wolves said they were coming over to the race when they woke up, and that they loved horses," said Brutus, honestly. "Met them in the forest last night, had a great party. Had a great fight this morning as well, fighting with all these people on chariots. Whipped em good though."

"The Werewolves beat Mars?" Zeus was astonished. "How did they manage that?"

"I organized them. They had no idea how to look after themselves, but when properly focused they pulled together and we all sorted out the crazy charioteer folk. Then we decided to come to the race." Brutus was quite pleased with the days effort.

"Certainly going to make the race more interesting," Zeus mused.

And just at that moment, who should come into the bar but Mars and Diana, along with Meridius (who was happily chatting to them about the state of daisies in the forest). "Hello Daddy," the pair chime in unison.

"I thought you were out hunting Werewolves!" he said.

"We were, and we are, but the bad news is that they are coming here, to the race. So we have entered into it. That way we can be on the field to catch them as they come for the horses. Hope you don't mind, Daddy, and while we would have preferred to surprise you, Meridius here said she saw that we had to come and let you know." Then Mars noticed Brutus, "And there's the bugger who made the dogs smarter than they should be! How in Hades name did you get mixed up with Werewolves?" he demanded.

"They are wonderful chaps," said Brutus, defending his friends. "And you were really sloppy. All they needed was a bit of organization."

To say things were a little tense was an understatement.

Stock it to Me

While the horse races were being planned up north at Bethel, Chincino had found excellent offices in the luxurious home of his former boss, Garum Marsala. Whilst initially objecting to the enforced occupation and threatening to call in the constabulary, the Patrician decided that the knife being held by Baraka Alashad that was very inconveniently at his throat was, in fact, an extremely good argument to the contrary.

"I hope you don't consider the actions by the OTHER person in this mix, the evil Claudius Hemus Spectre, to be tainting our natural and long lasting friendship, dear Baraka." he demurred as he showed them to their rooms.

Baraka just grunted. The pair had cheated him out of millions, and worse, it appeared they had absconded with most of his slaves. Speaking of which, those very same slaves all bowed low as their former master entered the room. At least they still had their lovely golden hair and blue eyes that the old warlord liked so much. He was starting to feel at home when he realized, dammit, that this WAS his home. He paid for it, and only put it in those clowns names to get around the non-Roman purchasing rules.

"Dear former boss, I am now a freed slave," explained Chincino to Garam, "and we are starting up a sort of accountancy practice here in your lovely Wall Street house. I know you won't mind that it is marginally illegal and only slightly putting you at risk of being thrown off the Tarquin Rocks."

Poor Garam, going from a poorly paid reporter at the New Rome Times to landed gentry had been to this moment a rather pleasing turnaround of events, but now all his dreams of sloth and living to an old age that was soaked in luxury were being crushed. "Why are you back at all? You know if anyone finds out Baraka is back in town, the creditors will be around snapping at his heels and off to debtors prison he will go. WHY are you disturbing my life!" he demanded.

Focus was in the prediction zone, flipping coins, then discussing things with Chincino, so there was only Baraka left to reply. He backhanded his former slave to shut him up, which only caused Garam to whimper. "We are here because you are next to the Stock Market and if you shut up, behave, and don't act like too big an ass, we MAY leave you this house and your life." The big African was in no mood to explain the technicalities of how they were going to dispossess the patrician thieves of their ill-gotten gains, in part because he didn't really get it, and otherwise because if was Chincino's business to sort out. The 'other' part of his disinterest in disembowelling Garam was the feeling he had in his bones about this new stock prediction idea. He sensed it would work, and Baraka LIKED the notion of making money.

Naturally, New Rome, though huge, was a small place for gossip. The whispers had already gone out that Baraka Alashad was back and looking for vengeance, and Claudius, the brave patrician that he was, had already escaped on the fastest horse he could find, for an important business meeting in Canadia. All the legal rights to property in the world won't help you when you are dead, he reasoned.

Chincino came out of the room where Focus had been coin flipping, and said, with confidence. "Orange juice!" A slave duly appeared with some lovely fresh orange juice, that he quaffed down, saying, "Yes, orange juice is going to be BIG! How much spare cash have we got on hand, Garum?"

Garum instantly understood that the question that referred to 'we' meant 'you' and was really a demand that roughly translated to, "Bring me all your cash!" He duly complied, not wanting to risk another close shave with a knife from Baraka. He reasoned that as he was still alive it was a good sign he might stay that way, but he was under no illusions as to how long that would last if he didn't do what he was told.

"Ok," said Chincino to all present, "This is the first test case, I am going to buy up Orange Juice futures, and spreading the word to all the buyers at the stock market that the Head Augury from New Rome is in a new business, stock prediction. Let's see if it causes a run and drives up the price."

Which is precisely what he did, coming back an hour later to report no instant movement. The stock traders listened with zero interest, because there had been no recent history of volatility in the OJ market, so just the word of the old man making predictions wasn't enough to spur them on. Then he had a thought, "Are you still working for Lord Rupus?" Chincino asked Garum.

Garum coughed, "Well, er, technically. I did tell him to stuff his job up where the sun doesn't shine, but I am still on the books as a reporter there. Why do you ask?"

"We need you to report a HEATWAVE that will strike tomorrow, a really bad one, certain to dry up the aqueducts it will be so bad. You got that?" Chincino asked/demanded.

"I will be hung by the coattails by Lord Rupus if I knowingly publish fake news that is genuinely fake," he protested.

"He publishes made up stories all the damn time!" Chincino said with a sneer. "This is just another one in a long line of them. Do it!"

Garum duly typed out a Raven about a terrible heat wave about to strike, quoting a portent or three to indicate the certainty of it. Chincino read it through, and suggested he add that Focus Maximus had subsequently predicted Orange Juice futures would go through the roof because of this terrible event. Garam duly added the addendum. He then sent it off, noting, "But just because I WROTE it does not mean it will get published. Lord Rupus inspects every article personally and he will wonder what the Hades I am up to and will then send someone over to beat me up to find out. I am only doing this because I don't want an immediate beating, but really, a beating is still on its way."

"Just send it," said Chincino. Now, having been Garum's slave for some years, Chincino knew everyone he dealt with in the New Rome Times. In particular, he knew the secretary to Lord Rupus, having had to go see her many times to clear up some issue with his former boss. "Ok," he explained, "Now I am off to see Maggie, his secretary. I am going to make sure this gets published in the afternoon edition."

ooo000ooo

"Maggie darling," he kissed her on both cheeks. "It has been SO long."

"Chincino, lovely to see you, and what delightful flowers. You were always the best slave that idiot ever had!" she exclaimed.

"Slave no more, my dearest sweetest Maggie," Chincino smiled his winningest smile. "Freed by Baraka Alashad and now his full business partner. We are working with the Head Augury, Focus Maximus, in a new business. You may have noticed a news bulletin to that effect?"

She looks puzzled, then remembers, "Oh yes, a Raven came in earlier. I had it here for Lord Rupus to go over, but he's out of town, at some horse race."

PERFECT! exclaimed Chincino to himself. "I wonder if he heard about the heatwave? But no matter, perhaps he won't mind that you didn't warn people, I guess. I am sure he will be very understanding that no one decided to publish that incredibly important information that could save lives, I mean, aqueducts drying up? Whoever could have imagined such a thing?"

Maggie looked closely at the article. "An article by your former boss, hey? Don't suppose you had anything to do with it?"

Chincino looked aghast, "What, me? No, I am motivated solely by the public interest, and er, perhaps by an interest in Orange Juice futures, and the run on them this article might create?" His one eyebrow suspended up in the air was enough to convey the real message.

"Oh, I see!" Maggie finally understood why Chincino was here. "This changes everything. Perhaps, in the public interest, this DOES need to go in. Orange juice futures, you say? Well, now that I think of it, Lord Rupus WAS intending to buy into those. In fact, so was I. And I don't suppose if he makes a whole lot of money he won't be too upset if this 'heatwave' doesn't happen as predicted."

"Just blame the Lead Augury and pocket the cash. I have missed you dearest Maggie," Chincino smiled once more. "And as it happens I am passing by the stock exchange on the way back home, because we are all staying with dear Garum Marsala for a bit. I would be happy to place the bets on for you both."

"Could you? That would make life so much easier. I will write you a chit for Lord Rupus' broker."

And so it was done. Obviously, as soon as the brokers saw the huge buy order for Orange Juice futures by Lord Rupus, the rush was ON. The price had gone up tenfold before Chincino sold out their shares in the late afternoon.

He then magnanimously gave back the money provided to them by Garum, only deducting ten percent, and smiled broadly at all present. "Well, that worked a treat."

Garum was not only incredibly pleased to still be alive, he even got some money back? Perhaps this might work out after all.

"Stock it to me baby, uh ha uh ha." he sang to himself.

A Curious Revelation

The God of War and the Demi-God Brutus (who was still entirely unaware of his status in the godliness stakes) glared at each other in a testosterone-fuelled eyeballing. Diana was the one who intervened, saying, "It was all good sport chaps. Settle down. We are here to sort out the wolf problem, not to argue with each other. So we lost a few of the heavenly host, and a few werewolves were sent across the Styx, it was still just sport! Remember that."

At this point, Rufus realized he had a question, so he put up his hand. Diana looked over at him, wondering what this speck wanted, and he took the opportunity, "I have always been very curious, we all know what happens to humans when they die, crossing the Styx and all that. But what happens when one of the heavenly host kicks it? I mean, is there a heaven above your present one where you go, or do you just evaporate into nothing? Because, if it were the later, then the option of being human is possibly a better one."

Well, there was quite an awkward silence. The bar had been emptied by all the punters who had gone off to bet on a donkey and all that remained were three Gods, two demi-Gods and an Oracle. "I mean," continued Rufus, 'I don't want to pry, but I am extremely curious about this."

Zeus broke the ensuing silence with a cough. "Ah, truth is, we don't know."

"You don't know? But you are Zeus, the chief God amongst the Gods. How can you not know?" Rufus was astonished. First the materializing of essentially useless items, now they don't know what lies beyond their own God-hood?

"Look, we know there is an underworld, my brother is in charge of it after all, but he only really got the job because he was such a complainer. We know there is a black river full of lost Souls called the Styx, and yes, my old mate Charan ferries you across, but let's face it, none of us really know WHY. It's something we inherited from the Titans, and weren't THEY trouble. Took ages to cast them out." Zeus snorted.

"Then why the Hades are we here at all, then?" exploded Rufus.

"Well, I like horses," said Zeus, by way of explaining nothing.

"I like hunting!" said Diana.

"I love WAR!" said Mars, proudly.

"And I love you ALL," said Meridius, ever the diplomat. "Look, honestly, trying to find reasons for anything only leads you to asking more questions about everything. It is what it is. People, and Gods, just take it as it comes. Take it all as it comes, day to day, and enjoy the ride, that's what I say."

Brutus had said nothing and was back to not listening to anything. Finally, he spoke, "Well, I just blew a motza betting on a donkey," he sighed. "I was never good at being rich. However (he brightened up) I did have a great party last night, so I guess that makes up for it."

"That's the spirit, I guess," said Meridius, kindly. "We have an hour till the race starts so I suggest we drink up, and get to our pre-race preparations."

"Oh," Rufus realized the time. "We have to do a pre-race show Meridius darling. Let's set up on the track, and as the donkey is in the race, we may as well bring him along so we can pack up quickly and get ready to roll as soon as it is over."

What the fashionable people wore to the Race

The Performance

The vast crowd had gathered. It was a huge spectacle and there were tens of thousands present. As big a crowd as any coliseum, Rufus noted to himself, and just as ugly. A lot of beer had been poured down a lot of throats and they were all murmuring in that special way that can so easily turn to murder.

The clowns came out, to a hail of rocks and various hard objects, and did their thing on the "Caesarian Bicycle" in honor of the great man who changed the course of Roman history. "How sweet," said Meridius. She loved Caesar and bicycles. Then when the clown show was done, they were on! Rufus had to admit, he loved this bit, with all the booing, the jeering and the insulting it entailed.

Here was the crowning achievement of his life, the thing he truly dreamed of: Standing in front of a large crowd, and telling them what disgusting slobs they really were. You prod them and prod them till they react and start to hate you. THIS was the true calling of the Un-Funny Comedian!

Look at you!" he called out, "You low life miserable curs of dogs scarving off from your work on a sickie to come to a horse race!" (They all cheer) "You lot are the most disgusting set of perverts I have ever met!" (They laugh and cheer) "I heard one of you had a wife that was so fat, that when she sat around the house, she sat AROUND THE HOUSE!" Boom, the punch line! It always took the really bad joke to get them going. FINALLY, he started to get the jeers and boos they were expecting.

After all these years of performing, he never tired of insulting an audience as much as they never tired of hating him.

"I went to a TINY TINY fortune teller the other day. I asked him how was business, he said 'Not good, because I have a bad habit of killing my customers.' Sooooooo I said to him, 'Does this make you a Small Medium at Large?' !!" NOW the rocks start to get thrown.

"You heard about the dyslexic devil worshipper? Sold his soul to Santa! (boos) Then he prayed to his DOG to get it back!" Many things were now being tossed in his direction. This was going well.

"You know, I once saw this small rock, then it grew and grew and grew, and I wondered what it was - Then it hit me!" (They throw more rocks)

"Ok people, now we get to what you have all been waiting for. This is Eruptus Non-Funnius, your Unfunny Comedians and here is the

DELPHIC ORACLE!" Suddenly the crowd is on their feet and cheering, apparently forgetting all about the leeches. Everyone still loved Meridius, the Oracle.

From out the back of the Donkey Cart emerged Meridius, all dolled up to the nines. Rufus forgot what a hot looking thing she could be, as most of the time she was being just Meridius. But when she came out in that tight fitting Oracle number, all sequined up, it made any man forget everything but her. She pulled out her python (Where does she keep it when not performing? Rufus never figured that out) and let it slither all over her, and THEN she brings out the Rubber Chicken.

The crowd roars at the sight of that famous non-chicken and she does her pretend ritual, spilling the rubber chicken intestines over the ground, and pricking Rufus' finger to put some blood on it. Then she seems surprised, genuinely this time, not as an act. "Ohhhhhhh," she said. "Big heat wave coming up!"

Well, she could have said Martians were landing for all that anyone cared about the prediction. It was Meridius the crowd loved and they roared and stamped their feet. "Oh Oh Oh Oh" they called out. It never wore thin, the Delphic Oracle was the STAR in upstate NewYorkium.

Now it was time for the cool down. Ofal comes on, looking like Ofal, and he has a banana in his hand. He holds it up to the crowd, then just sits down and start talking to himself.

As always the crowd goes quiet, trying to hear what he is saying. As the noise comes down, Rufus goes up and starts his patter.

"Are you talking to yourself?" he asks Ofal, though looking at the crowd.

"It is the only time I get a reasonable conversation" Ofal responds.

"It is a sign of madness," Rufus notes loudly.

"Majority-Minority Rule: Those in the Majority maketh the rules. But if the majority are stark raving bonkers, then the opinion of one of THEM is the notion of a lunatic." Ofal responds.

The crowd starts to mutter. They don't want a lesson in ethics or logic, they want blood and guts. So Rufus takes out a cymbal from the cart and starts banging it behind Ofal's head, saying "No one wants to hear THAT rubbish!" he exclaims! (The crowd roars!)

In response to the noise, Ofal takes the banana and squishes it into both his ears, going "Nananananananan ... I can't HEAR you!" (The crowd roars even louder, all the time while Rufus is banging on the cymbal)

Rufus urges them on, crashing his cymbals. "He says he can't hear you!" he is shouting at them now, and they are really getting to fever pitch, jeering, throwing things and generally abusing the idiot with the banana in his ears.

Ofal keeps going, ever louder, "Nanananananananananann - I can't HEAR YOU!"

More crashing of cymbals, more shouting from the crowd, until finally the crescendo is reached, and Rufus stops smashing the cymbals together. He then holds his hands for everyone to be quiet. They start lowering the noise, lower and lower, until all you can hear is Ofal, eyes shut, going "Nanananananan - I can't hear you!"

Rufus signals Ofal to silence by a touch on the shoulder. There is a dead calm all across the stadium, you could hear a pin drop, which is when Rufus delivers the almighty punch line. "And THAT, ladies and gentlemen, is why they call it a BANANA!

Ofal lifts up his hands and starts up with the "NANANANANAN" all over again, and NOW they pull out their instruments, Ofal on rhythm lute, Meridius on drums, with Rufus playing lead.

They bring on the latest, maddest and most crazy music ever to hit America, the wonder of ROCK and ROLL. "Nanan ana na na... I hear you calling, at my back door. I hear you calling right at my back door!" Rufus is singing, Ofal is singing "nananana", and Meridius is pounding away.

And the crowd goes INSANE!

Things start flying through the air at them, and at the crescendo, when the wave has peaked, they all head to the safety of the donkey cart and back to the start line of the race that is about to begin.

"I have to get over to Zeus' rig," said Rufus to the pair, "But damn fine job. They are really worked up now. It's going to be a great race. See you when it is over!" he shouts as he runs off, with things still flying in his general direction

Utter Confusion

The Gods had just left the bar to get to their chariots, the crowd was all at the track, and Eruptus Non-Funnius were already out there, performing, so there was only Brutus standing there, dejected. He had forgotten for a moment that he had put all the money on the Donkey, but now he remembered and all he wanted to do was drink. The race was nothing to him but a misery. He didn't know what he was going to say to his wolf brothers, he was such a failure.

He supposed, in retrospect, that the five hundred to one odds were a clue. He had thought it was just because Zeus' rig was such an outsider that no one ranked it. Now he realized the bookies had checked out the contenders and had made their own value judgment. So he just sat there drinking.

The bookies, of course, were delighted. A late surge had put ALL the big money on the DONKEY! They always thought the punters were insane but this just proved it beyond any argument. Then some of them started to get suspicious and sent people back to the stables to see what was up, which is when they caught Flavius doping all the horses with beer-soaked hay.

At last, someone had paid close attention to the late entry chariots and some bright spark asked if it was normal for horses to have wings. Well, a furor ensued out the back of the stables. "Look!" shouted Flavius to the bookies milling around, demanding answers. "None of it matters. I still have ... well, you know what ... and on top of this every damn horse in there has been fed beer-soaked hay, so ALL of them will be too drunk to win. And anyway, all the money is going on the DONKEY you fools. Whatever the Gods have done to smile on us like this, I have no idea, but they have. Stop arguing, stop bitching, and let the race run. We will all be rich in an hour!"

That made sense, so they went back to their totes and collected the last of the money being put down on the donkey. The insanity of people believing Zeus would be driving 'I am the Oracle', the donkey chariot, was just one more layer of the madness that had engulfed the race course.

Obviously, Flavius had given his motivational speech in front of very drunk horses. "Wha?" said one of them, confused. "I fought phis was supose ta be an 'Orse Race, not a DONKEY race." he said, slurringly.

"It HIS an 'orse race," responded another, equally tipsy. "Oi never signed up for no DONKEY Race! I fink that would be UNLEGAL."

"IL - ILLEGAL." One of apparently unaffected by alcohol Pegasus' commented from the Mars chariot. It is a little known fact that the winged horses are in no way affected by booze, in fact, they perform better with the odd dram under their wings. Some person suggested that the ambrosia of the Gods (curiously named after a red bull) is what GAVE them wings, but this is entirely speculative and possibly created by a marketing expert, thus most likely to be a complete lie. Theseus, the lead Pegasus for Mars who had just spoken was quite arrogant. He had no consideration at all for the feelings of lesser creatures than himself. "Where did you dumb nags go to school?" He sneered. Of course, he spoke in High Horse.

"Ooohhh." they all go in response. (bar the Unicorns, who remained silent and in the foulest of moods) "Some of us speak in 'igh 'orse do we? Ohhhh... So clever!" You may not have ascribed sarcasm to horses before, but let me assure you, they can be exceedingly so and very touchy about their lower class status, especially in relation to their more 'celestial' brethren.

"Orrr no, WE never had no wings to fly some Gods chariot. We common 'orse are just muck to you lot, aren't we?" said another nag.

"Yah, we is NUFINK to you lot are we? We are just NAGS and while we may not stand a chance against you in this race, we still have our PRIDE." There is a general murmur of consensus from the gathered horses, who were finally getting a beer-fuelled bravery to speak up.

The Pegasus understood their roles. Orion and Desponia, who were in charge of Zeus' chariot were there to win. Theseus and Polyphemus, in the Mars Chariot and Chrysaor and Charybdis with the Diana Chariot were there to hunt the wolves. These rather stupid common horse clearly did not grasp their role and purpose in this race, which was to be bait.

Theseus tried to explain, "Dear lesser cousins, perhaps I need to explain to you the true reason for you being here today. For one, it is not really about the race. You see, YOUR role in this days proceedings is to act as bait for the werewolves that are about to invade the course. I expect you will all die, but be happy! All this is for the noble cause of creating sport for the Gods."

As you might expect, this did not go down so well. In fact, just as the riders arrived to hop into their chariots and as the gates to each stable were being opened for them to proceed (supposedly in an orderly manner) to the starting gate, panic ensued. The horses may have been drunk but they were not stupid and accordingly they ran like Hades out of the stables, giving the appearance of an early start to the race.

This, in normal circumstance, would have been one of the worst possible outcomes for a race organizer. Yet, compared to a unicorn hearing that a werewolf will be present, this mad horse panic would soon be relegated to a mere incident. Which brings me to another small detail about unicorns, their horns ARE magical. They literally pop up when they get particularly excited. Being magical creatures, when they are given the correct stimulus their horn will re-grow in an instant. It is why the horn is worth so much money, and I would presume this gives you a clue as to their value and specific use in the medical profession

Foolishly, neither Master Rhodes nor Flavius understood the conversation between the horse and Pegasus'. Not surprisingly, they were extremely surprised that when the stall gates opened and their 'horses' sprouted horns, giving clear evidence as to what they really were. Not only this, the two sets of unicorns BOTH then ran out onto the field, snorting and snuffling in a very ferocious manner, looking for werewolves to kill. All thought of a race was gone and anyone in the chariots behind them were merely passengers.

And, as if on cue, seeing all the horses starting to run out onto the field, dozens of Werewolves then appeared from nowhere, leaping over the barrier to get their pound of horse flesh.

"This could get messy," Polyphemus said to Theseus. "We better call Zeus."

Right at this moment, a rather astonished Rufus turned up at the Zeus chariot and sees the utter confuddlement outside in the arena. He then asked the most logical question, "Where's Zeus! The race has already started!"

Race Riot

T he announcer for the race just presumed this was all part of the proceedings. "Ladies and Gentlemen," he called out, "I am your host, Rich Wrigley. Welcome to the inaugural Woodstockium Festival. As you can see, the contenders are lining up, and we have a few intriguing late entries. However, as you can see, the only chariot, if we can call it that, at the starting barrier is "I am the Oracle". This is the odds on favorite LOSER for the race, and for good reason. As you can see, it's a DONKEY!"

Now, most normal and sensible commentators would not announce a thing that would cause mass panic amongst the punters, but Rich Wrigley was essentially an idiot hired on the cheap by Flavius. He truly believed he was introducing brevity and wit to the event. What he 'really' said to the crowd was "Ladies and Gentlemen, you have just thrown all your money down the toilet!"

When the crowd realized that the donkey cart was the whispered 'sure to win' outsider, and that clearly Zeus was not driving it, they too surged forward to tear the poor donkey to shreds. So in the opening moments of the race, we have drunk horses running wildly in a panic out of the stables and onto the track, wolves leaping over the barriers to get to them, unicorns appearing from nowhere to hunt the wolves, and tens of thousands of people launching themselves at the Donkey, who fully understood that it had better get going, which he did.

Standing at the starting line, the race starter just stood there with his starter flag and presumed everything was underway, so he started waving it. At this point the Gods arrive at their chariots and realize the race has started early. "What the Hades happened?" Zeus asked Theseus.

"The common horses can't handle their beer," he replied, looking down his long nose.

"Dammit, who fed them beer?" he asked.

"Flavius came in and soaked their hay with it," said Polyphemus.

"How come I can understand everything you are saying?" asked Rufus, listening to High Horse and having it make perfect sense.

"You are a demi-God, remember," Zeus said with a sigh. "Oh, well, tune into the Unicorns and keep up. A race is a race, regardless of how it starts." Zeus then called over to his kids. "Mars and Diana, go kill a few werewolves before they eat ALL the horses."

And they were OFF, Rufus jumped into the chariot just as the pair of Pegasus picked up speed. But here the first chink in the logical sequence of events was made manifest. The Unicorns were not racing around the track, but zapping at an incredible rate of knots back and forth, stabbing wolves in the belly. It was extremely messy, but the Pegasus did what they were told to do, and so the Zeus chariot kept following them wherever they went, only it got to the wolf just before it was stabbed by the unicorns.

"Damn, this is fun!" shouted Zeus.

"This is nauseating," said Rufus, trying to hold onto his lunch.

To add to the drama, arrows were now flying through the air as the archers in the stands took up positions and aimed randomly at any wolf they saw. Only the wolf was rarely there by the time the arrow arrived, so really, there were just a whole lot of arrows flying everywhere.

However, as wolves pounced on horses, tearing into them, and as unicorns pounded on wolves, ripping them to pieces, and as everyone on the course avoided sharp, pointy flying sticks, the donkey kept running for his life from the crowd. The thing is, he may not have been able to outrun horses, but he certainly was quicker than people, and so he managed to stay ahead, while Meridius said soothing words, saying "Darling Donkey, it's not that they hate you, honestly. It is just that they have gotten all emotional over things..." Ofal just held on to the reigns and hoped for the best, while negotiating wolves, unicorns, arrows from Mars and Diana's support troops and the chariots of the Gods themselves, all the time staying ahead of the ravaging band of punters.

Now, dear reader, a question may have crossed your mind. *How come the wolves did not go for the donkey?* Well, this is because he was a donkey, and I have to say, it was a little dull of you to ask. Wolves like to eat Horse, and though they may not be the smartest things they certainly know the difference between a horse and a donkey, which apparently you don't.

At precisely this point, Trumpetus and Lord Rupus turned up. Seeing the madness out there on the circus, the cagey politician knew exactly what to do. Clearly, this was another one of his well-organized rallies, so he stormed up to the announcers box, threw Rich Wrigley out of his chair and took over the microphone. "Man," he says, with his cheeriest voice, "Hasn't THIS place gone to the dogs!"

Oddly enough, hearing the familiars tones of their future dictator caused the people to stop in their headlong rush after the donkey and turn to see who was talking. There, on a high podium, the Trumpetus was waving to them. They immediately forgot all about the race and the bedlam, and wanted to know what was up. "People, my people, so great of you to come here today to see me!" he bellowed out over the loudspeakers.

Did they come here to see Trumpetus? Well, he said they did, so maybe they this was the real reason they were there. Below him, the scene of utter carnage continued, wolves leaping on horses, unicorns stabbing wolves, Zeus himself zapping back and forth at the speed of light, while Mars and Diana were whooping with joy as they cut down werewolves all over the place. And all the time random arrows were falling like rain upon the circus. At this point, the people began to come out of the hate-filled rage that had taken them over and started to understand this was no ordinary horse race.

"It's a special day, and not just because I am here," said Trumpetus humbly, "But also because we are here together, with me. You know I heard about this rally and leaped onto a flitter with my junior counsel, Lord Rupus, just to come and speak with you all. I am here to make your life better, you know that. 100% of the people all know how much better their life will be when I am running things, so don't listen to that miserable 1% who say otherwise." The people nodded, impressed by the statistics.

A wolf was thrown high into the air, snarling and yapping as a unicorn jumped up to pursue it, apparently being preceded by two flying horse with a chariot behind them, and a quiver full of arrows. In all this, a very happy Zeus is shouting "Yeee Haaaa!" while the other very unhappy fellow in his chariot just held on for grim life.

"With you all here, I feel like I am talking to family, to the people who love me," Trumpetus was apparently oblivious to the carnage being performed in front of him, or perhaps it was just because he was quite used to it. "We have our ups and downs, but really, what we REALLY have is me, and that should be enough for all of you, because I am so wonderful. And Humble! I want to emphasis how humble I am." It is at this point that the donkey goes flying at full fear-fuelled pace right past the announcers stand, with Meridius quietly saying, "it's OK, no one is chasing us anymore."

But you don't get to be an old donkey believing that everything is fine just because someone says it is. They were still ducking wolves that were leaping through the air, as well as dead wolves on the track, bleeding horses that were running around crazily, and chariots shattered and broken all over the place. Added to this, the crowd was still on the track, albeit listening to the strange orange-faced human.

This is when the revelation struck! Donkey had an epiphany, a moment of clarity. He realized that this was a one-horse race, or rather, a one-donkey one. A few more laps and he would WIN this damn thing.

So it appeared that the only persons paying any attention at all to the race was the Donkey and the man at the starter gate who dutifully clicked through each entrant as they made their way past the lap counter, all the while ducking the odd arrow flying through the air. Now, given that the horses were all avoiding being eaten, that the unicorns were busy killing werewolves, and the Gods seemingly only interested in the party that was going on all around them, it was starting to look to the Donkey like he was the hot contender to win.

Only at that specific point, Lord Rupus pulls up alongside in a chariot, notebook in hand, asking questions about why the Oracle of Delphi had entered a Donkey into a horse race, and what deep portent did it signify? Meridius shouted a "Hello!" to Lord Rupus, and said what a lovely day it was. It was a little hard to hear things over the ruckus, so she indicated for Ofal to move closer to see what Lord Rupus might be saying.

"Oracle," he shouted. "Is this 'donkey in the race' connected to your stand on Leeches?"

"I never stand on leeches," she said, loudly and confusedly. "Why would anyone want to stand on leeches?"

"Then why HAVE you taken a stand on leeches?" Asked Lord Rupus, wondering if the entire thing about 'no more leeches' was Fake News.

And just as he thinks this, on the stand Trumpetus, who is still addressing the crowd, is saying "Fake News! All this about me and the Russians! All Fake News!"

"Fake news!" the crowd hypnotically answers back. "It's all Fake News!"

At this point, Zeus pulls up in his chariot, and Rufus shouts out, "We have got to get out of lockstep with these damn unicorns!" but just as he says this, another unicorn flashes by and the chariot is dragged off into its timeline all over again.

"Was that Zeus?" Lord Rufus asks loudly, trying to get over the roar of wolves, the shrieking of horses and the trumpeting of Trumpetus.

"That was Rufus," shouts Meridius back at him.

"That wasn't me!" Lord Rupus shouts in return.

"No RUFUS, he is the guy in the chariot with Zeus!" She clarifies.

"So it WAS Zeus?"

"No, it was RUFUS!"

Lord Rupus had many years of experience in field reporting, and he knew when a story wasn't running in the right direction. "This is all going in the wrong direction!" he explained.

Meridius was now definitely confuddled. "I am sure we are going in the right direction, all Roman Chariot races traditionally turn to the right. Do you turn to the left over here?"

"I never support the Left!" cried out Lord Rupus. "Unless it pays," he added.

All the while they are running round the ring, avoiding sharp objects, dead wolves, and broken chariots, and then, without any warning at all, a whistle blows, signifying the end of the race. The man had clicked through the Donkey to a full twelve laps of the circuit, so the race was officially over.

Now, here was the amazing thing. The man had apparently used a WOLF whistle to signify the end of proceedings. The high pitched tone of which cut through the werewolves blood lust, and they suddenly realized they were outnumbered and out-gunned with both Gods and unicorns after them. "Let's get out of here!" one of them shouted and on this call to retreat, the remaining wolves that still had breath in their body took off from the track, to make their way back to the underworld.

However, when they got there, the door was locked and bolted. But there WAS a sign pointing to ANOTHER door beside it, that read "IBIZA"... And this is why you will always find wolves with crazy hats drinking at parties on that strange little island.

Trumpetus saw all the commotion settling down and called out, "See? I am already making New Rome great again! Vote for me this election and we will all do fabulously better!"

There, amongst the carnage and wreckage, stood the dazed public, and as Trumpetus left the podium, Rich Wrigley gets back on, announcing the race result. "And the WINNER IS .... 'I am the Oracle'!"

A huge cheer comes up from the crowd. They are ALL WINNERS! Trumpetus really DOES make everything right! Back in the bar, Brutus hears the amazing news being broadcast. The Donkey won? Unbelievable... But he knows how these things work, you got to get in early to avoid the rush. So he runs over to the tote to find a dozen ashen-faced Bookies all preparing to leave in a hurry. "Hey!" he calls out, grabbing a large stick as he does. "No one leaves until I am paid, you hear?"

One of the bookies throws a pile of money at him and, as he stoops to pick it up, they are all off and running, because coming up from the field behind Brutus are thousands of drunk punters who all bet on a donkey to win a horse race.

Of course, the poor punters, never having experienced winning a race, had no idea how bookies react to large losses. There was much laughter and wild, frolicking sounds coming from a whole lot of winners holding their winning tickets, coming up to a place where no one would be around to cash them. Brutus, of course, thinks it is just another party, but he makes sure he gets the cash into a safe bag before it starts. That was a whole lot of Denarius he just got tossed. Enough to cover drinking for a whole year, or three, he reckoned.

"Where did they go?" asked a punter who had run breathlessly ahead of the crowd.

"Who?" responded Brutus packing the last of his money into a tote bag that had been left.

"The bookies, of course!"

Brutus then realized they had all mysteriously vanished. "They were here a moment ago," he said. But there, off in the distance, he could see them loading up their horses and getting ready to take off. At the same time, all the punters saw them escaping and, with a roar of anger, they all raced to find whatever conveyance they could find in order to pursue them. The next few minutes saw almost everyone from the race track piling into a huge traffic jam as they all tried to get off after the bookmakers.

Brutus watched them go and then finally realized, where did his wolfy friends go? They were supposed to be here.

Aftermath

Rufus was still reeling from the extreme speed of the chariot, but now the wolves were gone, the unicorns settled down, and Zeus' chariot finally came to rest. "Damn fine performance, that's all I can say," roared Zeus, apparently enormously pleased.

All around them were dead wolves and horses, the odd dead charioteer, and a whole lot of wrecked chariots. "Ah, I thought you liked horse," Rufus commented.

"Pfft, decent horses yes, but this lot were drunks. The main thing, we had fun, yes?" Zeus bellowed with laughter, waving over Mars and Diana, "Damn fine show!" he exclaimed, and the pair of them smiled broadly in relief. Their archers had finally stopped shooting random arrows, so it was relatively safe to walk about.

"Well, got to get back to Mount Olympus. Did you want to come along?" Zeus asked Rufus.

"Ah, another day. Feeling a tad queasy, chariot sickness and all that." Rufus answered, partly wondering what Mount Olympus was like, and mostly knowing he wouldn't like it

And just like that, the Gods take off in a ball of flame and fire, launching off into the sky, traveling over the clouds to get the speed up for the jump to Olympus. Not one miserable piece of gold or silver was left behind, just a field of Mars, littered with the dead and dying. Which was when Rufus realized he was soaked in blood, and that there were four sets of unicorn eyes looking murderously at him from the other side of the circus.

Behind them, a rather shaken Master Rhodes was barely in his shattered chariot and busily throwing up all over his wheels, while Flavius Corpus was experiencing an horrible realization: That money he had put on himself to win was gone. Damn, that Oracle had ruined his life AGAIN! So the poor man starts weeping. He was still weeping when the unicorns all decided they had had enough of these humans. Using their re-grown horns, they snapped their harness and took off to freedom, and to chase the retreating wolves.

Then Meridius and Ofal trotted up, the victorious donkey carrying the laurel wreath of the victor around his neck. "Did you hear? We won!" cried out Ofal, surprised at winning, but mostly surprised that they were alive. Even so, he was smiling and holding a bankers draft for five talents of gold.

On their way off the field, they came across Brutus, who was smiling broadly as well, waving hello. Despite his natural reticence, Rufus pulled up and asked if he was still going to New Rome, which he was, and so he may as well hop in - which he did.

"Well," he pronounced emphatically as he climbed on back. "I really thought we had no chance, but you have all shown me that I have been equinely prejudiced."

The Donkey, needless to say, was so simply overjoyed that he trotted along looking more like a pedigree stallion than a broken-down old donkey.

Amidst the ruin of his life and the ruin that was the horse race at Woodstockium, Flavius just sat in a crumpled heap, weeping, watching as Eruptus Non-Funnius, along with all his hopes and dreams, left him behind in the dust.

All he wanted now was vengeance.

Part Three: The Daily News

Whereupon all the cast assemble for a final soliloquy ... Printing is invented and New Rome burns, proving the wisdom of the prediction that came about with the end of animal sacrifice. And of even greater importance, we also come to the end of the book where it suggests yet ANOTHER sequel!

The Flaming Sky

All in New Rome saw the portents. Three flaming comets racing across the sky shining brightly in broad daylight. A tremendous wave of heat descended as the chariots of the Gods passed by and suddenly all felt an unquenchable desire for Orange Juice. Crowds descended on juice stalls, demanding the orange liquid.

Prophets started leaping up saying this was a clear sign from the Gods that they favored Trumpetus Orange. Real-world profits started leaping up as well, as Chincino and his fellows basked in the glory of a bull run on OJ futures.

Traders started clamoring for the next big tip, and dear old Focus Maximus was becoming aware that he had been given a new lease on life, because he, of all people, knew what the flaming chariots really were. He knew the augury and the signs and interpreted them to mean that the Gods themselves had blessed their new business! So he sat down with his coin, and asked about more stocks, carefully writing down the Gods response (via the coin) to his questions.

He liked the new gig. It was much cleaner work than gutting chickens and sheep, and SO much more scientific.

The happy troupe were out of Woodstockium and on the Via West Hurely, to connect to the 82 that took them to New Rome. Happily trotting along in their cart, pretending to listen to Brutus ramble on about some great thing he had done during some war somewhere, Rufus had the thought to ask Meridius, "Ah, the leech thing, here in New Rome no one wants to kill us as yet. Do you think we could keep the whole prediction thing a little quiet? I mean, we are nicely cashed up and I would really like some peace and quiet to spend some Denarii without getting murdered."

Ofal nodded, he had forgotten all about that. "Oh, well, I have to say I agree with Meridius on the whole leech thing. The more I thought about it, the less sense it made. Someone had a cough, leech them. Someone sneezes, leech them. Really, it IS pretty damn stupid."

This was the moment that Meridius chose to pull the eyes rolling in the head thing. and talk in a strange voice, "My children are to go to the house of Garam Marsala and speak with Focus Maximus!"

"My children?" quizzed Ofal, "And Focus Maximus is at Garam Marsala's house?"

Rufus sighed. The voice of Apollo speaking through his chosen instrument presented the rather large elephant in the room he could not avoid. "OK then," he started saying grudgingly, "I have a bit of news. Zeus mentioned it in passing that, apparently, Brutus and I are indeed half-brothers and also the children of Apollo. So, Brutus and myself sharing a last name was NO coincidence."

The guttural voice speaks once more through Meridius, "Oh, no it was pure chance that you both had the same last name." And then Meridius was back to herself, entirely unaware of what she had just said.

"Your voice said we have to go see Focus Maximus at Garam Marsala's house," explained Rufus. "Oh, and Brutus and myself are brothers, and Demi-Gods."

"That's nice," said Meridius, slightly more preoccupied with a lovely hedge they were trotting past.

Brutus was so busy talking to himself that he heard nothing at all, "And of course, there was the time fighting the Albigensians in the South of France, damn those women were TOUGH!"

Rufus was not entirely sure that anyone took his Demi-God status seriously. It was not the response he had been expecting but he was glad Brutus didn't hear. They may well be related, but the boy can go relate somewhere else, preferably far away.

"The Oracle at the games said we would have a heatwave tomorrow," Ofal commented. "We should invest some of our money into ice."

Again Rufus is surprised. Ofal had business sense? He not only organized the performance, now he is talking investments? What a topsy turvy world! But he had to admit, it made sense. The price of orange juice on roadside stalls had already doubled, so ice would be the next thing to go up. "How do you think they manage to get the ice down from Canadia before it melts?" he asked, offhandedly.

"I saw them using barges loaded to the gunnels with furs over them to keep the cold in." Ofal mentioned.

"I thought you used fur to the keep the cold OUT." answered Rufus.

"One of the mysteries of science," Ofal said wistfully. "I always wanted to be a scientist, you know."

"What stopped you? Family couldn't afford the university fees?" Rufus asked. He had never known his sidekick to have any interest in anything but where the next meal was.

"No, just too stupid," he said.

"You are not really stupid," Rufus suggested. "This idea about investing in ice is a good one, though I have no idea how you invest money into something that melts so quickly."

"Maybe we should invest in furs then?" Offal said, hopefully. "Though it would seem the opposite of what we should invest in with a heatwave coming up," he added, answering his own question.

"Investing was never something I understood," Rufus agreed.

Ofal wrinkled his brow and then made up his mind to ask, "Is it true you are a demi-God?"

"I am glad SOMEONE noticed," answered Rufus. "Apparently, and I am also supposed to be Brutus' half brother. Zeus said it, mentioning that was why I could ride in his chariot. I still wanted to throw up, though."

"Do you suppose you have any special powers ... Like Heracles, maybe being super strong?" Ofal was not skeptical, more just confused.

"Nothing that I have noticed," Rufus blew out between his teeth, shaking his head. "It all seems a bit overrated, really. I mean, there we were with Zeus in our cart, and did he really seem so special?"

"Well, he did manifest some horses and other stuff," Ofal noted.

"And what USE were they? I mean honestly, what use are the Gods themselves, really? For all this myth and legend we learn about in school, they forget to mention how the Gods were entirely disinterested in US. Zeus only hung out because there was a party to go to. As you know, I have always being a little skeptical over the whole thing, now I am entirely clueless as to why anyone is important or anything is anywhere." Rufus was feeling a tad depressed. Perhaps it was coming down from all the excitement, or perhaps he realized that being a demi-God was not really anything special at all. Much the same as discovering you were a carrot and that the only person who liked you was a donkey.

Ofal nodded. "Very Existentialist," he said.

"That's a big word, what does it mean?" Rufus asked, curiously.

"No idea," Ofal answered. " I heard it somewhere and asked someone to define it, but no one seemed to know what it meant. So I gathered it means things you didn't get. There was a fellow, a philosopher, you know, one of those guys who makes a living selling air. (Rufus nodded) Anyway, he said it meant that a tree could fall in the forest and no one cared. I presumed he wasn't talking about the timber milling fraternity. However, I DID note that people used the word when things made no sense, and when everything seemed entirely pointless."

"VERY existentialist," replied Rufus.

"Isn't it just," responded Ofal in agreement. That seemed to finish the depth of conversation they wished to plumb and so, as the donkey trotted proudly along, for many an hour after that they sat in silence watching the scenery go past, all the while listening to Brutus drone on in the back about some great battle he had with an ox.

The Green Door

The home of Garam Marsala was noted for two things. One, it was beside the Stock Exchange in Wall Street, and the second, it had a large, wooden door that had been painted green. It was late at night when Rufus found himself knocking on that specific door and was quite surprised to find one of Baraka Alashad's slaves answer it. He was even more surprised to find Baraka who, he had heard, was on the lam from creditors specifically because of the investments he had made with Garam Marsala, was also there, and that everyone seemed to be getting on fine.

"Come in, come in," said Garam. "Focus made a prophecy about you lot and leeches, and apparently the new business venture going on here is going to make a fortune out of it. I have no idea how it all works, but it's a far more sensible way to use prophecy, predicting ways to make money."

Meridius went in to embrace Focus, then paid her respects to the other men in the house. Rufus and Ofal were very pleased to be offered a beer, while Brutus sat and had some late night food, talking as he did about some out of the way cafe' he had found in Istanbul and how wonderful the Kefta was, though camel milk was not to his taste.

The Donkey was stabled and watered, but a keen donkey observer would swear his ears sat more upright, as if the fellow had discovered a far greater sense of pride in who he was. And indeed, when the horses in there heard about him winning at Woodstockium (horse whispering was a far more reliable source of news than the New Rome Times) there was no looking down the nose. Instead, he was accepted without any insults, indeed, even regarded rather well. Whoever heard of someone outrunning a unicorn AND beating the Gods at the same time, after all?

"We read about the amazing race at Woodstockium, where your Donkey beat out all comers," said Chincino. "It was the lead story in the New Rome Times this evening and there has been a great deal of buzz about how the Oracle must have cheated, because a donkey cannot win a horse race."

"No mention of Zeus or Mars, or Diana? No mentioned of winged horses, unicorns or the bookies running to escape the crowd after them to collect on their bets?" Rufus asked, astounded.

"Not a word," said Chincino. "Were the Gods connected to the three comets that crossed the sky, the ones making everything hot?"

"I imagine so," said Rufus, dolefully. He was wondering if his demi-God status was ever going to be recognized, because apparently a donkey winning a race is more important than a God, so what chance did HE have? None. Now he felt really depressed. It is one thing finding out you were a demi-God, but entirely another to gain any sort of respect for it. He really felt like throwing a tantrum, which was a very non-demi-God thing to do, he felt, so he didn't, because no one would care anyway.

"Oh, while you are here, a small detail of making the business arrangements between myself and Baraka Alashad official. It needs Meridius to sign it, in her role as the Oracle." Chincino added as a passing thought. The Oracle wandered in, smiled, and signed the paper after which Chincino breathed a sigh of relief. All this work and only NOW was it official he was a full partner.

It was the early hours of the morning when, finally, they all sat down in the lounge to have some beer and talk about what had happened to them since they last met at Flavius Corpus' house. There they all were, Meridius, gazing off to some other place as always, adding the odd polite, "Uh Huh" to the conversation on odd occasions. Focus was also rather distant, constantly flipping his coin and muttering to himself, while Brutus talked to no-one in particular, as usual. Baraka and Garam had already fallen asleep. This left Chincino, Rufus, and Ofal to do the catching up.

"You see," explained Chincino, "Baraka and myself are now full partners in market trading. This new business is brilliant because it holds nothing, pays no rent, has no staff, and no-one can repossess it if things go bad. We buy nothing but the potential of something, which is recorded as being ours on a piece of paper - And it can't go off because it is paper."

Rufus thought it sounds like witch craft. "So you own nothing but a promise, and you buy and sell that promise on the promise of greater or lesser promise to come?"

"Pretty much," agreed Chincino. "We are really in the prediction without the messy need for cutting off chickens heads. We predict what will happen to the value of a commodity like Orange Juice, and lay bets on what we think it will be worth."

When Rufus heard about this new *predicting what will happen and make money out of it'* business, he started wondering about the question that had vexed him since leaving the horse race, "Well, how would we make money betting that ICE will be more expensive?"

"Excellent question. Well, the first thing we must do is to create a product called 'Ice Futures', then we predict what these 'futures' will be worth at some point in the future. Then we bet on how accurate our guesses on this might be ." explained Chincino.

"So, am I understanding that to invest in Ice, the thing to do is to NOT invest in ice, but in what it's future will be?"

"Exactly," said Chincino, happy his student was grasping the concept so quickly. "And a good thing, because ice melts so quickly, whereas its potential in the future is entirely reliable."

Ofal was now interested, "So the whole trick to making money in this new world is to not put anything into any REAL thing, only bet on what you IMAGINE it will be worth later on. So we are really betting on imagination!"

Chincino was entirely happy. "You chaps will make excellent market traders, I can tell."

Baraka had woken up with the talk about his favorite new subject, playing with the market. He chirps in, saying, "I have no idea how or why it works, but it works and Chincino here is very good at making sure it works. But did you say Ice, why Ice?"

Rufus explained, "Well, logically, there is a heatwave, people will need ice. As it will melt more quickly coming down from Canadia, there will be less arriving while more people will want it, so the price will go up."

Chincino rubbed his chin. "Makes sense," he said. Then he turned to Focus and asked, "What do the Gods say about ice, Focus?"

The old man took out his coin, bit it, then flipped it up and seeing the result, nodded approvingly, "Good, very good."

"That settles it, tomorrow we create our OWN product on the stock market, Ice Futures, and we lay down some bets on what it will be worth next week. My guess is that the price will at least double, maybe triple."

"How do we bet on something that hasn't happened and isn't actually real?" asked Ofal, curious as to how it all worked.

"Well, we use a BROKER. In this instance, we use our newly registered broker, dear Garam here. He is now the official broker for our new company, called 'Bitcoin'. You like the name?"

"Because Focus bites the coin before the prediction?" suggested Rufus.

"In part, but also because we will make quite a bit of coin over it," answered Chincino. "Plus it is a catchy title, people will remember it."

"So what does the broker do?" asked Ofal.

"Well, essentially nothing. He takes money and, like a bookie, writes you a chit. He then puts the money into a large box called a FUND, which is a strange name because no one ever has any fun in there. The thing about betting on futures, it is a Zero-Sum Game. The amount of money WON is equal to the amount of money LOST. The trick is to be on the winning side. The money goes into the box, and bets are placed on a particular item, in this case, ICE. People bet the price will go UP or DOWN at a certain point in the future.

"But it has practical, real world uses. Let's say you are a butcher, and you need ICE to keep your meat cool. You see the heatwave and, being smart, you want to lock in the price you will pay for ice four days away, when you will need to buy more. You take out a FUTURES contract offering to buy a ton of ice at fifteen hundred. As an ice importer, you think this is a good deal, this is 50% above current market value, so you accept this contract and agree to provide a ton of ice for that price on Thursday." Chincino looked at Ofal and Rufus. Good, they were getting this first stage.

"But now it gets complicated. Ice starts going up to Two Thousand, and so the contract for fifteen hundred looks really cheap, so someone might offer to buy it from the butcher for seventeen hundred. The butcher figures he has made two hundred and maybe can stretch the ice in his shop for a few more days, so he sells the contract. You still getting this?"

"Sure," says Rufus, "just trading, but on what things will be, not what they are. But the guy who bought the ice off the butcher has no use for it. What will he do with it when it arrives?"

"Precisely. HIS trick is to offload this ice at eighteen hundred and NOT take possession of it. So he sells, and some silly shuck in an accountancy firm thinks, '200 under market value? I will take that!'

The whole point it, no one ever gets their hands on the ice. We sell the PAPER VALUE, not the actual ice." Chincino checked they were still following.

"But it gets MORE complicated, because some OTHER bright spark places an entirely different bet on top of the bet already made on ice. He creates a 'derivative' which is a completely imaginary stock, and bets on the future of these ice futures. And on top of this, people are laying side bets as to the day when the price of ice will go up or down." Chincino concludes his basic introduction and sees the confused eyes before him.

Rufus says, "It sounds completely crazy, but I love it! It's like betting on what cockroach will get to the edge of the table first, then betting that you bet was right, or wrong. However, the heatwave will pass and the price will go back down. What do people do when the price drops?"

"Who cares! We made our money, now all that melting ice is their problem," says Chincino with a shrug. "But, in the end, the people who are actually buying the ice have a use for it and let's face it, they all knew it would have melted by Monday and be utterly worthless."

"That sounds completely insane!" Says Ofal. "What you are all betting on is ICE, which is effectively a bet how much cold water will be worth tomorrow!"

"PERSACTLY! Now you are getting it," laughed Chincino. "First thing tomorrow BITCOIN will be registering some Ice Futures!"

"Ice!" roared Brutus, suddenly enthusiastic and returning to something akin to a general conversation. That's what I want, some ICE in my beer! Brilliant notion, who would have ever thought of it? Ice in BEER! I love it! I remember when I was in the North of Canadia, looking for that gold mountain, when I wrestled a bear ... Loads of ice up there."

It was at this point everyone realized Brutus was soaked to the eyeballs with booze, "But where's the ice? You were talking about ice just then. I want ice!" At which point everyone ALSO realized he had actually vaguely heard something someone else had said.

Focus Maximus came out of his coin flipping for a moment, saying, "Brutus, wonderful to see you are with us at last."

"Do you have ice?" Brutus points a finger accusingly at Focus, indicating a suspicion that HE might be the one hiding it from his beer.

New Rome Times

L ord Rupus looked proudly at the headline: 'DONKEY WINS BIG
RACE!' Now THERE was real journalism. On the spot reporting,
live from a chariot, talking to the Oracle and being right there when
the impossible happened. He ordered one of his secretaries to pat him on
the back.

"Um," she asked cautiously, "What happened to the other horses in the
race. They weren't mentioned."

"Stupid girl, that is why you are a secretary and I am rich. No one cares
who comes second. The ONLY thing that matters is who came first. Only
the winner matters, that's the story, everything else is unimportant." Lord
Rupus snorted.

"But, some punters who were there came in complaining that they
weren't paid by the bookies, and they wanted to place an advert as to
where to find them. THEY said there were werewolves jumping onto the
track, and unicorns, and even Gods in chariots chasing the unicorns all
over the place," she said.

"And what of it? Did any of them WIN? No. Yes, I know, there are
always side lines to the big story, but the REAL story, the thing people
NEED to hear, is that a DONKEY won a horse race. It is a world first,
something that has never been done. Remind me never to promote you to
a journalist, now get out." Lord Rupus was upset that someone was
dirtying up his perfect headline with facts.

Before she scampered, she dropped the note on his desk, the reason she
was there in the first place. He frowned at the sealed parchment. Special
report from Erik Britain, the fellow who sent him the note to get up to
Woodstockium. Could be interesting. But when he opened it up he knew
he would be getting upset over the contents because the headline ran,
"Publicity seeking bitch in sad attempt at PR for failing concept!"

Following this terrible headline ran a diatribe about how the Delphic
Oracle had contrived a stunt by putting a donkey in a horse race, and
wrote DISPARAGINGLY about her and the donkey. How DARE he go
out of his way to contradict the boss! And then he notes all the
information about her 'ringers' being paid actors, designed as part of a
stunt to get media attention.

Now that he thought about it, there WAS a great deal of kafuffle going
on in the background, but he presumed it was all part of the entertainment.
For a moment he considered the thought that maybe it WAS a publicity

stunt, but realized he could not have gotten it so wrong and that it was already printed anyway, so therefore his version was the truth. "Fire Erik Britain," he said into his pipe that led to one of his secretaries. There, he felt better already.

He sent the wasted papyrus to the 'pit' - the place where all failed news stories were delivered. Nice picture with it, though, of the actors with the oracle. No matter, to the pit with it all.

The PIT

Several days had passed, and ice futures soared as predicted. As a result, BITCOIN was rapidly attracting attention from a small cadre of investors, but anything sent to Lord Rupus for publication, essentially stories to promote the business, had been discarded. Even when Chincino went to Maggie to try and get things across the line, she shook her head. "Everything you send in goes straight to the Pit," she explained.

Instead, the headlines were about a shepherd girl who found a spring, and about how an aqueduct was being built right away, to cover for all the ones that were disappearing. The next day was an article on the miracles of aqueduct development, with a small footnote on the ever-increasing price of ice.

Not a word about the spectacular profits and performance of BITCOIN and, like it or not, without free publicity the general public would not be getting onto the bandwagon. This was where the real money was to be made. Garam was waiting outside when Chincino emerged, "Everything is being sent to the Pit," he said which, as everyone knew, meant it was never to be seen or heard from again.

"How are we going to tell the story of BITCOIN to the world?" Garam asked. "Lord Rupus owns every news sheet in the city and, unless he comes onside, I don't see how we are going to get out to the public."

Chincino looked to the heavens for inspiration, "Let's go to the Pit and see what is there. We might be able to write out some of your reports and leaflet the city with them, try to get some interest that way."

When they arrive, it was unguarded. I mean, who guards a fire trap like the Pit? It was essentially a large stone room full of parchments carrying stories that failed the editorial standards of the New Rome Times. Garam picked up a few, including the odd one he himself had written in times past. "Damn, there are a LOT of stories here," he said.

And there, right on the top of the pile is the latest discard, the beautiful painting of Mars, Diana and Meridius, with the winged horses of the Gods AND the Donkey in the background. Chincino is drawn to it, for no particular reason, then he smiles. What a brilliant bit of inspiration! Absolutely Brilliant! Suddenly inspired, Chincino grabs the painting and gazes at it for quite some time. Then he says, "Let's come back here with the donkey and load it all into the cart. I have an idea."

ooooOOOOOoooo

Back at the Wall Street house, Rufus was entirely obliging in lending out the donkey. Given that ice futures had tripled and then quadrupled their winnings from the race, he was feeling rather generous. Inside an hour, he and Ofal, along with Garam and Chincino were parked outside the Pit, loading up the cart with all manner of parchments. "What are you intending to do with all of this?" Rufus asked as they made their way back to BITCOIN HQ, as Garam's house was now called, and which the garish new sign outside the residence now read.

"I have had an astonishing notion," said Chincino. "It was triggered by that painting of the Gods and Meridius. Not the Gods, but how your donkey in the back ground had been stamping his hoof. I saw that he left the perfect replica of his hoof print in the hay. I said to myself, 'Self, Lord Rupus is powerful and almighty because he can afford thousands of scribes to write out his parchments every day' ... But when I saw the hoof print, I was struck with a brilliant idea. Tell me people, if you dipped a donkey hoof into ink, and it stepped onto a papyrus, you would see a perfect copy of his donkey-shoe. Yes? "

Rufus didn't see where this was going. "I imagine so, but why would anyone be interested in a donkey hoof print?" (The donkey snorted, slightly aggrieved) "Sorry Donkey, but it was not aimed at you specifically."

"But what if, instead of a donkey hoof, I carved a Latin letter, dipped it into ink, and stamped THAT?" Chincino asked.

"Obviously, you will see that letter."

"And what if I carved the entire alphabet, and arranged it into words, what would you see?"

"The words, of course. You would make a print of whatever words you had arranged with the letters. I don't see how this helps us, though." Rufus was a little confused, but Garam was getting the picture.

"I get it!" exclaimed Garam, who was far more experienced in the publication business. "We don't need SCRIBES, we need CARVERS, but surely it will take longer to carve a story than to write it?"

"Only for the first one. Then we can ink it up, place a parchment over the top, and press it. Then we can do another print, and another, and another. We could put out THOUSANDS of parchments for the cost of one carving. Gentlemen, I have created PRINTING! It will be the greatest tool for propaganda, I mean news, ever invented!" he exclaimed, clearly excited.

"All well and good," said Ofal, "But all that parchment will cost money and why would anyone want to read it?"

"Oh, I get it now!" said Garam suddenly getting the whole concept. "That is the point of the stories. I am seeing where you are coming from, you are going to recycle all these stories and reports Lord Rupus discarded and use them to fill out the parchment with interesting stuff. And it will just happen that in the middle of each parchment will be a story about how well BITCOIN is doing, what a great investment BITCOIN is, etc."

Chincino was grinning from ear to ear, "PRECISELY Garam. All those stories are a virtual MINE of interesting tales from all over New Rome. Plus we can do a daily prediction about the weather, people are always interested in that. We can get Focus to predict if it will rain, or whatever, the next day. All the farmers will buy it just for that!"

"Brilliant," shouts Garam, truly excited, "We will call it 'The Weather Report'! And right beside that we can do another prediction called, 'The Stock Report' which will be about the stock market and BITCOIN! And what about (he is getting really excited) a way to PAY for all this. We have the FLIP side of the parchment printed as well, where we list everything that people are wanting to SELL. We can say it is a special section, a CLASSIFIED section."

"Love it," says Chincino. "Garam, I am hereby appointing you as the new editor in chief of ... what will we call this thing?"

"Well, it is news we will be delivering daily, I presume, so why not the 'Daily News'?" suggested Ofal.

"Perfect. An oblique throw-away towards The Daily Muse that Lord Rupus runs. He will hate us all the more." said Chincino. "The 'Daily News' it is!"

When they returned home, the carvers were already there and setting up in the stable. The carpenters were also working with a hastily drawn blueprint that Chincino had given them, which was basically a table with a large, flat wooden plate suspended over it, with a wine press screw to drive it towards the table. The excited entrepreneur explained to his fellows what it was all about.

"You see, we put the carved wood-block stories in here (indicating a frame on the table) and then we ink the top, placing a sheet of parchment over it, then we screw down the plate to make sure it gets even pressure all over, and VOILA (Using Gaulic words now?) we PRINT our first parchment for the 'Daily News'" They all applauded.

It took a few days sorting out details, like carving everything in reverse. They even invented a printing script, a pun on the New Roman Times, called Times New Roman. (very nice serifs) And THEN Rufus had the brilliant notion of carving each letter separately and placing them into a grid. This meant you could use the same carving over and over, and just rearrange them into a box grid. Then they had the next notion of doing a whole story in one section, and placing various sections together to form what they called a news sheet

It all worked rather well and inside a week they had their first publication, a News Papyrus is what they called it. The thing sold for a single sestertius, and they went like hotcakes. The biggest attraction, artists could carve PICTURES and they could be printed as part of the news story. Revolutionary stuff, and a quarter the price of the New Rome Times.

Obviously, such an incredible step forward in news technology had to be protected, and so Brutus was employed as security. He duly beat up anyone who came up to the house, including the mailman, until it was made clear he was only protecting the printing presses and the stable grounds. Whereupon he finally came across someone who was genuinely interested in everything he had to say, the Donkey. He had trotted out for exercise and ended up helping Brutus patrol the grounds.

The actual truth was, of course, that the Donkey was being particularly friendly only because he was high as a kite on printing fluids and, believing he was now a Pegasus, he thought he was flying around the grounds, not walking.

The Orange Principle

Trumpetus Orange was fascinated by this new phenomena that was gripping the city. The heat wave was starting to abate and people were finally slowing down on murdering unwanted relatives who had over-stayed their welcome. It was beginning to be cool enough to hold another rally, though he had to say, the one at Woodstockium was particularly brilliant.

It really annoyed him that Lord Rupus ignored the whole reason for going there and published that a stupid donkey won a race. Anyone can rig a damn race! Look at him and the consular elections? That was already in the bag with appropriate bribes. No, the real story was now about his incredible speeches. "I got the best words," he said to I-trumpet, his daughter, who nodded graciously. "I got all the best words, but what use are they if Lord Rupus doesn't publish them?"

But this Daily News thing had his interest. Maybe he could bribe them to publish his speeches? He turned to his daughter, "I-trumpet sweetey, my cutest and bestest ever thing I ever did, apart from all the great things I have done, but you know that... Could you trot down to the office of the Daily News and pay them some money to print my speeches?"

She was a good girl, and jumped up to do exactly this, holding out her hand for the chariot fare. "How much is the offer?" she asked.

"Just argue for whatever you can get it down do sweetlips. I need to have the people know how incredible I am, but Lord Rupus is being a craphead and hogging my limelight. If I didn't need him on the ticket, I would fire his ass right now."

She nodded and took a chariot. She understood that, at its heart, she represented a very important thing, a point of DIGNITAS generally known in the family as "The Orange Principle". This was the principle where Trumpetus Orange got everything he wanted, regardless of principles. And if he got everything HE wanted, she got everything SHE wanted. She also knew that Baraka Alashad was hiding there while he negotiated his release from debt and she had been quite fond of his parties in the past. This would be her 'in'.

ooooO0OOoooo

Chincino sat with Baraka while I-trumpet pitched the notion of printing her father's speeches. He was sitting there wondering what mileage he could make out of this beyond a mere bribe. Baraka was doing the talking, however. "But your father is partnered with Lord Rupus?" questioned Baraka. "Why don't you get 'him' to publish your father's speeches?"

I-trumpet looked coolly at the two men, sipping her wine. "Very nice wine," she complimented them. "In fact, it is SO good that it tells me you want more from this visit than a mere bribe to print speeches."

Unlike her father, Chincino realized, this one was smart. Straight to the point AND accurate. He opted in to the negotiations. "Yes, we may have a mutual business interest, which is that your fathers' marketing empire could be of great use to us. As you know, present in this house is the Oracle of Delphi. As you will also know, she has predicted the end of leeches in medicine, and generally decries bloodletting in general. Yes, I know, very un-Roman, but so much of New Rome is changing and this is just another step."

He paused, letting her comment, but smart girl, she says nothing. Just sits and listens. At this point Meridius waltzes in, and smiles broadly, "I-trumpet darling, how good to see you! It has been years since Delphi, how's your brother?"

"Behaving now we locked him in the study, but just as dumb. Is it true, Oracle, that the use of leeches will end?" I-trumpet came straight to the point, she could smell a business deal.

"It is what I have seen, my darling. I have no idea how it will come about, but Rome as we know it is gone, and the world will not stop changing. Leeches and bloodletting have had their day." Meridius stated.

"But what will replace them?" I-trumpet asked. Ah, the look in Chincino's eye told her THIS was what the meeting was really about. Looking right at him, she asked, "YOU have something to replace leeches?"

Chincino smiled broadly, and brought out his little satchels of white powder. "This has all the properties of leeches, but no biting involved. We call it ASPIRIN, an extract that comes from plants. It reduces fever, thins the blood, takes away headaches, to name just a few advantages. In short, everything a leech can do without the expense of a doctor calling, or the inconvenience of anemia."

"OH," she says, impressed. "Have you got a good marketing name for it? I can see one right away, we could call it WHITE POWER! You know, a pun on White Powder."

Baraka coughed, "Possibly not the most sensitive name," he suggested.

Chincino covered. "What I was thinking of was associating it with SEX. As you know, the main excuse for avoiding sex that a woman offers is that she has a headache, well NOW all a guy has to do is pull out a little packet of Aspirin, and she will be good to go! I am thinking we give it a name that gives the message without having to actually say it - like BEX."

I-trumpet nodded. A good name. "What do you want from my father?"

"We publish his speeches, and what's more, we will criticize them, and say terrible things about everything he writes. This GUARANTEES people will read them, because it looks like gossip. But he has got to say the most outrageous things, like building a wall between us and Canadia, and we will keep saying how terrible it is. This will make everyone buy the newspapyrus, because nothing sells like gossip. We will have a section of the publication specifically for politics and elections." He looks up, she is clearly liking what he says.

"In return, you and your father will start spruiking ASPIRIN, and retail it through all your stores. You will make the usual retail mark-up, of course, and we will give you a franchise for this. There is millions to be made, but even better, the NEXT miracle drug we have in the wings will make ASPIRIN look like a kids toy. It is a GOD POWDER, and anyone taking it believes they become a GOD... It is called Cocaine."

"I have to run it by Daddy, but I think he will go for it." I-trumpet nodded. This was another way of saying she would make sure he agrees. The deal was as good as done. "Oracle, I believe you have changed the world yet again."

Meridius just smiles, "Pardon?" she asked. She had gone off into some other place and had already forgotten everything they had just said.

Baraka explains to I-trumpets quizzical look. "She is barely of this world I-trumpet. Her body is present, but she comes and goes. It is the nature of the Oracle."

As she leaves, the African prince turns to his partner and says, "Very clever. We have just bought ourselves immunity from prosecution. Lord Rupus will find it difficult to lock us up in courts while we have his senior Consul on-side."

"On the subject of courts, I have ALSO almost resolved the creditor issue," Chincino noted. He was trading futures with creditors in order to release his former boss from debt and, using his own Roman citizenship and the BITCOIN profits, he was also getting the real estate holdings back. As agreed, Garum was going to keep this house but the 'other' Patrician, Claudius, had taken off. They were having to hunt him down. In the meantime, the fellow was doing a fire-sale on his properties. (an unfortunate name, given the heatwave) Fortunately, however, BITCOIN were presently cashed up and buying the lot, so the escaping Patrician was inadvertently doing them a favor.

News Wars

Obviously, Lord Rupus Murdochius noticed the declining sales of his fine publication and the subsequent rise of this upstart Daily News. He realized that Trumpetus must be backing it, because why else would anyone bother to publish his terrible speeches? But he had to admit, clever ploy, publishing them in full - then insulting them, saying what utter garbage they were. People were climbing over themselves to get the latest edition, while they were leaving all HIS news sheets in the hands of the street vendors.

He knew precisely what direction this was going in! He needed to get into this printing business, which meant he needed their technology, which meant he had to smuggle in some artists to paint what was in their workshop. However, the brute they had on guard duty, along with the insane guard donkey with him, seemed to be on watch 24/7.

He had already employed assassins, but after a few came back with more bones broken than a sacrificial horse, it was hard to get anyone else to try. What he needed was a different strategy, a way to get IN, and then he had a brilliant notion: he would pretend to be friendly!

It had been a mere few weeks since Trumpetus had done deal with the Daily News and there was Lord Rupus himself, turning up at the door of BITCOIN. He had the general notion of getting in the door by offering to invest in this new-fangled printing idea, purely to get the information on how it all worked, of course. He hated business partners, they always seemed to think they might have ideas worth having. No, he would follow the ancient adage, 'If you can't steal it, you have to buy it'. (Which was not an ancient adage at all, but something he worked out for himself)

"Hello!" he said, very brightly, as the door opened to the BITCOIN house in Wall Street. "Is my dear friend and still current employee, Garam Marsala in?"

Ofal had answered the door, vaguely recognizing the fellow as the one who was on the chariot interviewing Meridius during the horse race, so he shows him to the sitting room. As he walks into the house Lord Rupus is craning his neck, looking for clues about this printing thing, but the surroundings were devoid of any information. "Garam!" Ofal calls out as he leaves.

Needless to say, Garam arrived and was rather shocked to see his former boss smiling. Seeing his Lord Rupus in his house was one thing, but smiling as well? That was truly dangerous. "How might we help you

Lord Rupus?" he asked, holding his money belt to make sure it wasn't being snatched. Even as he asked the question, he could feel an existential crisis happening, as if the tree that no one saw falling in the forest was being sawn up by malicious carpenters.

"I was wanting to chat with Baraka Alashad and Chincino, I think there is a great future in what they are doing." Lord Rupus said, laying cards on the table. "As you were once a loved and cherished employee I felt you were the person to approach in this matter." The smile that followed was the best any crocodile could muster.

Garam nodded, so Lord Rupus was here to steal their printing press. "It is entirely a matter for them to discuss. Are you happy to wait while I pass on the message?"

Garam went to the next room where Baraka Alashad and Chincino had been listening. They went to a quiet corner to discuss things. Baraka opened the conversation, "Well, he will find some way to steal it whether we let him in the door or not. I say the best solution is one that makes us the most money before he gets his hands on the concept."

Chincino agreed. "We need to delay things until we are set up with Aspirin. So we ask for unobtainium. We say that we will give him everything he wants, but we ask for something he can't get. That will hold him off for a bit. The truth is, BITCOIN is rolling and inside a few months we may well have more cash than Lord Rupus. We only have to delay him until the printing press business is a second string to the bow. The real question is, what can we ask for that he can't provide?"

"Humility?" suggested Garam.

"Certainly unobtainable, but it has to be something he believes he CAN achieve, but which will take him a lot of time to find. Not something completely impossible," said Chincino.

"Open and fair coverage of news and events?" suggested Garam.

"BRILLIANT!" said Chincino. "Perfect. We can say the only partner we will consider is someone who is ethical, honest and upright, with only the interests of the people as their guiding light. He can't sit there and say he isn't all of this, because this is everything his rag says it represents. We can pick any story they publish for the next year and find some sort of breach of our high standards."

"Isn't that just a tad hypocritical, considering all we wanted to do was promote BITCOIN, and were perfectly happy using his rag to begin with?" said Garam, apparently being afflicted with a slight case of ethics.

"Of course it is hypocritical! And your problem with this is?" snapped back Baraka and Chincino in unison.

"Well, all this means is that Lord Rupus will know it is a stalling tactic. Might I suggest a subterfuge UNDER the subterfuge?" Thus is was that Garam put forward his own brilliant plan, based on his experience using Focus Maximus as their proofreader in the news room.

So it was settled, they file back to have the conversation.

ooooOOOOoooo

Baraka cleared his throat, and sombrely started the proceedings. "Lord Rupus, we have considered your request, and instead of rejecting it out of hand, we feel we can bring you in as a partner in our latest endeavors, but only if you agree to meet the high standards of ethics and morality the Daily News represents to its readers."

Lord Rupus continues to smile, though gritting his teeth just a tad. He knows a setup when he hears it, but he HAS to have access to this new invention. So he is patient.

"Yes," continues Chincino. "As you have trained Garam here, personally, in the fine art of journalism, you would already know the exacting standards of truth and honesty that would be expected. Conscientious reporting of the facts, punctilious and painstaking researching of background to each story, and an unflagging dedication to revealing the minutia behind each claim the newspapyrus prints. This is what we need to see in our partner.

"Now, as these are already the standards by which the New Rome Times operates, I am sure you will have no difficulty agreeing to these terms as a condition of partnership?" Chincino concludes.

Rupus was wondering where the trap is, this was too easy. "Of course," he agreed in the same way a cat agrees to eat food put down by a stranger, "there would be no objection to this. As you rightly point out, this is already the stated mission of the New Rome Times. So the real question comes down to how much you want?"

Baraka smiled his best carnivore smile. "Oh, we have loads of money. It's not about the money, what we NEED is a trustworthy partner, such as yourself, who can expand the operation, for the good of the people. So I trust you will not mind if we bring in a third party, one who is a specialist in the requirements we have noted, to verify that these exacting standards have been met."

Lord Rupus now knows when he is being made the bunny, but he has to ask, "And whom might this ethics police person be, may I ask?"

Chincino smiled, good he has taken the bait. "Someone well known to you, a person we can both trust completely, our dear friend, Focus

Maximus, the Lead Augury of New Rome." Now, no one had actually asked Focus if he would do this, but all present knew what a persnickety fellow he could be with both punctuation and ethics.

Lord Rupus realized this was the hurdle he would have to cross if he was to get his hands on these new printing presses. He had to accept their spy into his camp. "And how LONG might be this review process take?"

Baraka holds out his hands, palms open and upwards, showing his best welcoming attitude, "Dearest Lord Rupus, a mere three months, a period where we can safely come to terms with the editorial standards we all know should be achieved, for the public good." He smiles, then continues, "Obviously, this is a probationary period, but I promise you we will have the good grace to offer an extension should there be any sort of grievous breach of ethics, for any reason. Oh, and in the meantime, I will also need Roman Citizenship."

Ah, finally! This was the real issue! Baraka was sick of having to work through underlings to do business in New Rome. Well, this WAS going to be expensive. A lot of people would have to be bribed, and certain protocols followed. "Done. But first, you will need to take up a position in the military, an appropriate one where you will counsel the officers in battle tactics. You will have to wear the uniform and play the part, and it will be expensive. I presume I have to foot the bill?"

"Of course," smiled Baraka. "And joining the army poses no problem."

"Then consider the deal done!" said Rupus, happy he got away with it so cheaply. They had him over a barrel, and the only alternative was the crossroads assassins solution, which because of that damn guard they had that option was looking less likely. They shook hands and Lord Rupus left. He was over the moon, imagine, being friendly actually worked? He was grinning from ear to ear and positively felt good about life and his place in the universe.

As Garam, Chincino and Baraka watched the chariot that brought him wheeled out of the courtyard. They stood there, waving Lord Rupus farewell. "He thinks the hard part will be the citizenship," said Chincino, laughing.

Persnickety Perfection

Nothing like this had ever descended on the venerable halls of the New Rome Times. The scribes hated him. They truly and deeply detested this evil man who made them do and redo EVERYTHING. "The comma, no that is wrong. You don't add a comma before an 'and' unless you have bracketed a phrase leading up to it with commas," said Focus with the patient authority of a man who knows his grammar. "I know you find it difficult, but correct punctuation is the heart and soul of good Latin. Now, go back and do it again."

It had been six months, SIX MONTHS of this torture, and every day some new problem was found. Some scribe somewhere made some small error and it had to be corrected. "If you allow ONE spelling mistake, one example of poor punctuation to escape," said Focus to the staff that collectively wished he would get run over by an ox cart, something some had already arranged, but being an augury he foresaw it and sidestepped the event. "You let just one thing go by and there is a question in the mind of the people from that day on. They will ask themselves, *'Was 'accommodation' spelled with two M's' or one? Did Millennia have two N's or just one?'* It is our sacred duty to ensure we do not create these quandaries in the minds of the public!"

Focus was rather surprised when he was called up to assist Lord Rupus in improving his publication. It had already been his job correcting the engravers, who he was sure loved him for it (They hated him as well, of course) but it was SO much more complicated when you have a thousand scribes to sort out. However, one day soon he was sure they would finally get it.

Lord Rupus was pulling his hair out. This was not what he expected, punctuation and spelling? The old coot was so fastidious and he just kept finding mistakes. But, despite the frustration, he had to admit, the New Roman Times WAS beginning to attain an incredibly high standard of Latin. Maybe it WAS for the best? But in the meantime, Hades looked like a vacation spot. And those scribes could complain all they liked, once he got his printing press they could all go to Hades!

One thing Lord Rupus was learning, we was learning how MUCH he needed printing, because all you had to correct was ONE plate, not a thousand different scripts from a thousand scribes.

"And here, you have slipped from past tense to present tense. And you have ALL done this, not noticing that the original transcript had the error.

Tut tut, seriously, after six months you are STILL getting tense muddled up? Do it AGAIN!" There was a collective groan across the floor, but they had no option, if they wanted to be paid, they had to make the old man happy.

Returning home that night, Focus was perhaps the happiest he had ever been in his life. It wasn't just the luxurious place he had to live, so much nicer than his hovel out in the sticks. Now he had new purpose and an important role to play, not just with predicting the correct stock futures, but in correcting and adjusting the very substance of what the people read every day. He went right to work on the Daily News when he got back, checking the engravings for the morning edition

"We have had people sniffing around," said the lead engraver. "Brutus knocked them senseless, of course, but we have also had people talking to our wives, asking about how everything works in here. They are offering money ..." he added, a way of indicating he wanted to be paid more.

"Really?" said Focus. "Well, speak to my nephew. He is in charge of security."

Focus, of course, was clueless as to the not-so-subtle threat he just made to the fellow, who went white and said, "Oh no, none of us would ever dream of taking money to tell Lord Rupus how all this works!" he exclaimed.

"After all," added Focus amicably, "Once he gets his own publication up to the standards we hold here, Baraka and Chincino are GIVING him everything he needs to know, so it seems odd that people are asking questions."

The carvers and engravers put their heads down, and just worked harder on the next days' headline, "ASPRIN, the WONDER DRUG!"

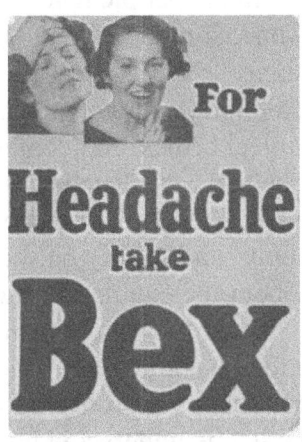

The Orange Revolution

Trumpetus Orange: Home of the Trumpinius Rex: This is what the sign said over the top of every single one of his shops. There was no actual NAME for the business, the business WAS Trumpetus. Some people said it was vanity, others explained it was a brilliant marketing ploy based solely on brand awareness, but the vast majority didn't care what it said, because inside they could get Aspirin. It really was the wonder drug, so much so that the doctors surgeries were largely empty and their leeches were starving.

Further, the staff at the medical centers were quitting, not through boredom but because THEY were now the ones keeping the leeches alive.

Trumpetus had now been elected as Consul, along with Lord Rupus. Of itself, the position was a nominal appointment where their only real task was running the yearly games at the coliseum. However, Trumpetus decided that the Senate wasn't really up to expectations, so he gave them speeches on how to do things right, every day, for hours on end. The cunning plan worked and soon enough, they stopped attending, which left HIM the business of running things, which he liked.

For the most part, Trumpetus was genuinely happy with his circumstances. For one, if he was rich before Aspirin, now he was disgustingly, astonishingly rich. The partnership had gone better than expected and all was well with the world.

Plus, and more important than money, he was now truly famous. People were yelling and shouting at him wherever he went, calling him names like 'DICTATOR'. What better proof than you have been effective in this world than to have so many people hate you? The only problem was that, for some unknown reason, there were also people who seemed to think he should DO something.

They clearly misunderstood the entire reason he wanted to be Consul, which was to look good, collect bribes, and do absolutely nothing. And even more annoying, now he had Lord Rupus constantly whining in his ear about his deal with the Bitcoin people. I mean, that was HIS business - nothing to do with Lord Rupus' and ideally he should keep it that way, but the fellow kept on and on about the egalitarian right of the people to a free press, etc. etc. which really meant he wanted their press.

He was being pressured to DO something, which he didn't like at all. "We need to pass a law about obstruction of information" Lord Rupus had been saying all morning. Didn't he understand how much the Trumpetus didn't care? Plus, these people at the Daily News were making him a fortune, why on earth would he want to rock the boat? But Lord Rupus was this continual mosquito interrupting his otherwise pleasant day. Finally, he agreed to do something, which was to go and see the lads down on Wall Street and talk about a way to shut his junior consul up.

The lads had a very simple technique of dealing with Trumpetus. They essentially ignored him and gave the job of speaking with him to Rufus.

Surprisingly, Rufus got on with the Trumpetus very well. He seemed to take the man's bluster and bragging about how great he was as par for the course. Whenever the fellow started saying things like, "You know, I have a huge brain, a colossal brain. I have the best brain in the world." Rufus just nodded approvingly. As a result, Trumpetus found that he really liked Rufus. He became the natural 'go to' person for all their business arrangements, which was curious because his arrangements were with Baraka and Chincino.

However, none of this mattered to Trumpetus, as long as everything worked out in his favor. Given that nothing he ever suggested or said to Rufus made the slightest difference to how Chincino organized things, it was thus far a perfectly amicable arrangement for all. "You see," explained Trumpetus, "Lord Rufus is an arse. He is a lying, thieving SOB without an ounce of scruples, which is why I like him, of course, but it can get tedious. He is all excited and keen on getting access to your press, you see, and he won't stop going on about it. Do you think you could give him one, just to shut him up?"

Rufus just nodded in agreement. Trumpetus took that as an excellent sign his troubles would soon be over and started to explain his program for New Rome as the Senior Consul. "You see, I call it the Orange Revolution. This is when the power is removed completely from the people and I put on large and expensive entertainment to distract them. Then I make myself Emperor and they won't be concerned because of all the shows I will have on every night."

Rufus just continued to nod. "And as Emperor, we can do away with all the time-wasting and inefficiency of the Senate, so that will save the State a lot of money as well, and by the State I mean myself, of course. This means there will be far less people I have to bribe to get anything done, so it will be more efficient all round."

Rufus, of course, just nodded. He found the way Trumpetus' hair bobbed when he got excited was fascinating. He didn't care about politics, or know anything about it, so whatever the man wanted to do was fine by him. What he DID hear was the bit about more entertainment which meant more gigs and he was getting itchy to get back out in front of the people again. "Shows EVERY night, you say?" Rufus echoed enthusiastically.

"Every night and even some matinees!" exclaimed Trumpetus, happy to have a convert to his cause. "Everyone will make lots of money, especially after I enslave anyone who can't meet their debts because then slaves will be cheaper as well. We are talking luxury lifestyle here."

Unlike Rufus, who was presently nodding enthusiastically at the notion of more shows, Chincino was sucking air in through his teeth. He had been listening in behind a screen and recognized that their new partner could be turning into a business risk. Tyrants, once installed, had a nasty habit of not honoring obligations, such as payment for goods received. Well, maybe it was now time to shift the tide to the other side of the political fence.

"Lord Trumpetus!" Chincino walks in smiling and confident, addressing Trumpetus with a thoroughly undeserved noble honorific to set the tone. "How wonderful to see you. I was just thinking about you and the incredibly healthy profits you are receiving as a result of Aspirin. How goes it, and what might we do for you today?"

Needless to say, when presented with effusive praise, Trumpetus lost all ability to think of anything other than how wonderful he was. Which Chincino knew, of course, so he kept right on rolling. "I can only say what a pleasure it has been to have you as a partner and might I say, you are looking very trim and fit today. Have you been working out?"

"Well, not so much. It must be my good genes," responded Trumpetus, finding his voice enough to demurely and politely turn the compliment to his parents' genetics.

"And good common sense, dare I suggest? Here you are, senior consul of New Rome who so NOBLY and WISELY remains so kind as to visit lowly commoners such as ourselves, as if you were no better than any of us. Your humility astounds me, especially given your huge talents and vast grasp of business."

Trumpetus just smiled. What a pleasure it was to visit these young lads, so friendly, so wise. Then he remembered why he was there, "Ah, Lord Rupus has been getting antzy over the publication thing. He really wants IN, and I was wondering if we could throw him a morsel to shut him up?"

Chincino spread his hands outwards, palms up, making an open display of honesty that only the best crooks can fake. "Well, we CAN, if you INSIST, but you know all the free publicity we have been giving you will become diluted with too many other publications out there. I don't suppose he has given an undertaking to print, then ridicule, everything you say?"

Trumpetus stopped and thought, something he rarely did. "Good point. Very good point. But you know how slippery he is, we will need an undertaking from him to do this, won't we?"

"If you say so, I will accept your wisdom on the matter," said Chincino. "And I agree with you. I feel that if he were to guarantee to slag off at you on a regular basis and insult you with ridiculous cartoons, then there is a possibility we can finally share the necessary technology. Do you think he might go along with it?"

"He will have to if he wants to be able to learn about this printing thing!" exclaimed Trumpetus.

"Well, in that case, I suppose we CAN oblige and help him out, only because you insist, of course." Chincino smiled warmly. "I will call a meeting and get the ball rolling right away."

Trumpetus left feeling he had proven once more just how smart he was.

However, Chincino knew that when Lord Rupus was informed of Trumpetus' plans to overthrow the Senate just how this would play out. What it really meant was that the Trumpetus was going to toss the junior consul onto the dung heap. There would be no need for any agreement to openly ridicule the Trumpetus - But this way, Lord Rupus would bear the heat, not BITCOIN.

"Did you hear?" said Rupus with a cheery note that future employment gives all actors, "We are going to have more entertainment."

"Yes," said Chincino sarcastically. "Just what we need."

The Mad Parade of Bacchus

Trumpetus made good on the promise of more parties in the street. In his plot to take total control of New Rome, there was a never-ending stream of distractions and bribes. What it meant was that nothing was getting done and that, instead of working at their insignificant tasks, the plebs were rolling around the streets completely plastered. Life was a constant celebration, a mad parade of Bacchus.

Countering this, Lord Rupus, now he had printing presses, was swamping the streets with diatribes against the Senior Counsel, inveigling the people to rise up against his tyranny. Well, seriously? What would you prefer? A party with lots of free booze or someone in your ear ranting constantly with dire warning of things to come? The plebs laughed at the New Rome Times, and Trumpetus became the most popular figure ever to attain the dictatorship of New Rome.

The Senate was discarded, democracy was officially proclaimed a nasty little popularity race, and the Trumpinius Rex finally lived up to his name, he became the King of New Rome. But what did it matter to the business class? They only care about their money and with no government restrictions, they all made a fortune. Money flowed like honey.

And what did the people need for all those hangovers from all those parties? Aspirin, of course. Baraka got his citizenship, claimed back his rightful property, and he and Chincino became rich beyond the dreams of avarice. The stock market boomed, and BITCOIN became the darling of Wall Street.

"Aspirin will cure all the problems AND it will replace leeches?" Baraka laughs, "I am starting to like all this New Rome Age crap the people believe in!"

All would have been fantastic, except for a small detail. The Christians! They sat there, nursing their torches, cursing the new age of Rome where they were no longer beaten up, picked on, or sent to the lions. What purpose did they serve? In this new world, no-one cared about them enough to be bothered. Well, they had a plan and they were not going to be ignored any longer!

"A good fire will sort this out! People need a reminder of the HELL they are bound for if they don't change their ways!" roared the priest who called himself 'The Shepherd'.

New Rome Burns

As Trumpetus could not play the violin, he had someone high up in the Trumpetus Insula play it for him. Wild chords spun out of control from the crazed fiddler who, if you looked closely, seemed to have small horns, and were those hooves he was wearing on his feet?

The offices of BITCOIN were not under threat. Despite the fact that most of New Rome was burning Chincino had foreseen the danger of fire and had already gone to extreme measures to protect the property. Because of the printing press, they had so many flammables in the stable. In order to protect this investment, he had already organized for water to be pumped up from the Hudson for emergencies such as these. This water was currently being sprayed all over where they were.

Meridius, Rufus, Ofal along with Focus sat on the porch, looking at the great orange glow in the sky. So appropriate, given the man responsible for it. Baraka and Chincino had come out to join them, while Garam had gone inside with Brutus to bring out more beer for them all to drink. Finally, the whole troupe sat down together in a rare silence, watching it all happen. This was when Rufus suddenly remembered how Meridius had predicted the end of New Rome. Turns out, it wasn't the ending of sacrifice, it was insane Christians needing attention.

"It has all come to pass." he said with a noble gesture largely fuelled from the contents of his wine glass. Feeling the true weight of the situation, he sighed and nodded, saying, "The end of New Rome."

"Do you think Trumpetus will claim this as a victory for the Orange Revolution?" asked Ofal.

"I think Trumpetus will be buying up real estate up at fire-sale rates," noted Chincino ironically.

"Not much of a fire, really. I remember ages ago, in Londinium. Now THERE was a fire," said Brutus.

Finally, Rufus tweaked, "Ah, the great fire of Londinium was three centuries ago, Brutus. Did you really remember it, or did someone tell you the story?"

He looked a little puzzled. "I remember I got hit on the head, woke up and everything was fuzzy. Funny, I only remembered it all just now, looking at THIS fire," he said, distantly.

Meridius smiled broadly, "And my dear sweet Heracles, are you finally beginning to remember who you are now?"

Rufus' jaw hit the ground, and he turned to Focus, "Isn't he your nephew?"

"Something like that," Focus said wanderingly. "Brutus ended up on my father's doorstep some eighty years ago, or thereabouts. Said he came from a relatives place in Old Rome, a cousin of mine. I sort of assumed that made him a nephew. Funny thing, he looked just like he does now. Some people just never seem to age."

Brutus looked up at the sky, "Heracles? Yes, I remember that name. It DOES seem familiar, now you mention it."

And then as if one shock was not enough, through the raging fires of New Rome a new fire emerged! It came with a roaring, bellowing sound which followed a flaming chariot that had two black Pegasus leading it.

The magnificent and now familiar rig pulls up in front of the BITCOIN house, and Zeus leaps out, shouting, "Am I late for the party?"

From the stables, in the stillness and shock of the Gods arrival, the happy sound of a positively enthusiastic donkey echoed brightly:

"He Haw, He Hamed, He Honkered"

After the Fire

Obviously, the insurance business was in tatters. Companies were filing for bankruptcy left, right and center. But more importantly, the houses that were left burned without any insurance company covering their loss which meant they were going for a song. Chincino was well-positioned with his new business partner to collect many properties.

Eruptus Non-Funnius were rich, and the Oracle once more proved her veracity as a soothsayer because the success of Aspirin pretty much killing the Leech market. Clearly, this made BitCoin the blue ribbon investment of the decade.

Finally, the medical profession got on board, not with Aspirin, but with the fabulous invention called COCAIN. It was discovered to be the worlds greatest nasal decongestant and given the terrible rash of sinus conditions after the fire, it became the cure of choice for most people. Soon after, it became the drug of choice for everyone.

It didn't even matter if you were sick, people queued up at the doctors' office for their daily snort. With all these profits rolling in, no one cared about Leeches anymore and the entire medical stock was sold off to poor African farmers, who thought they were buying tasty snails.

Zeus stayed on for a bit and pretty much drank dry Garam's entire supply of alcohol, but Garam no longer cared because he was alive where, by all rights, he had expected to be rowing a boat across the Styx.

Then, one day an extremely tired Raven turned up with a message for the Oracle.

"Come to Delphi STOP Strange new Sulphurous Fumes needs decoding STOP Oracle needed STOP"

Next: Rome Tor - Wear the Fox Hat!

OLD HARRY JENKINS

A SCOUNDREL CAN
MAKE A DIFFERENCE

This is a short tale to warm the heart. Available as an E-Book or hardcopy from Amazon. A first class story from a first class story teller.

Old Harry Jenkins is released from Prison, aged Seventy. He has nothing to look forward to, no savings, and his friends are all dead. There is only his son to collect him from the prison gate.

He has a bleak future in front of him, yet all the kind things he had done for others in his youth were about to catch up. This little book will fill your heart and stay in your thoughts for years to come. A pure little gem.

A Fabulous Short Story by Michael Wallace

About the Author

Ecallaw Leachim is considered by many to be a polymath. He is accomplished in many diverse fields, as a Master Musician, Master Body Worker, Master Numerologist, Dice Master, Recording Artist, Songwriter, and Publisher. On top of all this he is also a prolific writer with over seventeen titles in print.

Ladder to the Moon Publications

www.laddertothemoon.com.au

Aiming for the Stars is much easier if we stop off at the Moon. We are then out of the atmosphere of our past, and can see things more clearly. We are lighter, can jump higher and further than ever before, and it takes far less energy to start each journey.

The hard part is climbing that Ladder to the Moon.

Rome Tree

A funny thing Happened on the Way to the Horse Race

COPYRIGHT 2020 Ecallaw Leachim

ISBN: 978-0-6484277-5-9
Copyright 2020 Ecallaw Leachim
Publisher: Ladder to the Moon Productions
Email: qrcaustralia@gmail.com
Web: www.laddertothemoon.com.au

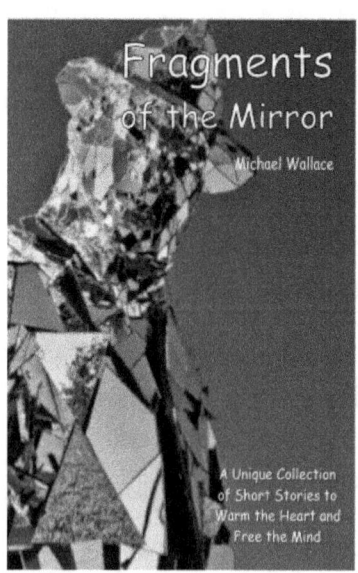

Fragments of the Mirror

Delightful vignettes by this author

If you enjoyed this story, you will love the collection to be found in "Fragments of the Mirror". You will see parts of your life reflected in the many stories in this book.

Available on Amazon
http://goo.gl/vgWA7n

EXCITING NEW BIOGRAPHY

PSYCHIC NAZI HUNTER

A TRUE TALE OF AN INCREDIBLE LIFE

Written from extracts and articles provided
by his son, Dr Cyrus Wood-Thomas DC

A Biography by Michael Wallace

"AN ASTONISHING STORY THAT HINTS
AT WHAT LIES UNDER THE SURFACE
OF WHAT THE PUBLIC IS TOLD"

www.ingramcontent.com/pod-product-compliance
Lightning Source LLC
Chambersburg PA
CBHW072030170626
46811CB00008B/3018